LOVE ON A BARREN MOUNTAIN

by

WANG ANYI

translated by Eva Hung

— An Authorized Translation —

A *Renditions* Paperback

© The Chinese University of Hong Kong 1991
All Rights Reserved. ISBN 962-7255-09-2

This translation first published 1991
Reprinted 1992

Renditions Paperbacks
are published by
The Research Centre for Translation
The Chinese University of Hong Kong

General Editors
Eva Hung   T.L. Tsim

Printed in Hong Kong

LOVE ON A BARREN MOUNTAIN

Contents

Introduction ix
Chapter One   1
Chapter Two 41
Chapter Three 93
Chapter Four 141

For Women Who Love Not Wisely
But Too Well

Introduction

Wang Anyi was born in 1954 in Nanjing and brought up in Shanghai. During the Cultural Revolution she was sent down to Anhui province, where she joined a local performing arts troupe as a cellist. She returned to Shanghai in 1978 and became an editor and then a full-time writer. The winner of two national literary prizes for fiction, Wang Anyi is one of the most prolific Chinese writers of the last decade.

Love on a Barren Mountain is the first of three novelettes, popularly known as "Three Loves", written by Wang Anyi between 1985 and 1986. It was first published in the Chinese literary magazine *Shiyue* (1986 No. 4), and earned for its author immediate critical acclaim as well as ideological criticism. Sexuality and extra-marital affairs have always been taboo in Communist China, so it is no surprise that Wang Anyi should have been criticized in 1987, during the anti-bourgeois liberalization campaign, for violating such taboos. However, since the praise has also centred around the subject of sex — the "Three Loves" have been labelled, quite unjustifiably, *xing'ai xiaoshuo* or "sex fiction" by a number of critics — Wang Anyi's other fine qualities as a writer have been overlooked. In fact the "Three Loves" have much more to offer than one writer's bold adventure into the forbidden grounds of sexuality; equally apparent in these stories are the author's keen powers of observation, her interpretation of the roles of men and women in love, her evocative lyrical prose and her sense of humour.

Love on a Barren Mountain is based on a true story. The cellist in the story was Wang Anyi's colleague in the Anhui performing arts troupe; in the orchestra the two of them shared a music stand. However, the real-life story only serves as a starting point for the author's exploration of human nature and human relationships. It is Wang Anyi's belief that in any love affair, women are stronger than men; this is particularly so when they are faced with emotional crises. Such a perception of the relationship between men and women is apparent in Wang's earlier short stories such as "Fallen Leaves of Gold" and "The Road to Shu is Hard" (1984-85); in the "Three Loves" it is unmistakable. The hero in *Love on a Barren Mountain* is not only emotionally dependent but physically weak, and the story is drawn to its inevitable conclusion because his lover and his wife, each so strong in her own way, completely dominate the ineffectual hero.

The story is not a romanticized account of an extra-marital affair. This is nowhere more obvious than in the last scene, where the hero follows the heroine to the barren mountain to commit suicide. The heroine is wearing her favourite white dress and high-heeled shoes; the hero is in a vest, shorts and slippers, carrying a shopping basket. The sense of incongruity in this scene underlines Wang Anyi's perception of the love relationships in the story:

> They [the heroine and the hero's wife] were fighting for a weak, cowardly man, a man who was in fact not worthy of their love. But when a woman loves a man, it is not for himself but for the realization of her own ideals of love. For these ideals a woman would give everything; she would sacrifice herself.

These words are perhaps most revealing of Wang's perception of the source of women's strength in love. However, the incongruity mentioned above also serves to emphasize Wang Anyi's success in gaining our sympathy for the lovers, for the reader is made to overlook this incongruity and concentrate on the emotional intensity of the characters' predicament. Thus, without trying to romanticize the story, Wang achieves a sort of transcendence through banality.

Like *Love in a Small Town* and *Love in a Beautiful Valley*, the characters in this story have no names; they are simply "he" and "she". It is as if their existence as individual characters is second in importance to their roles as the embodiment of a devastating, but common, emotional experience. And although the author seems to place the story in a number of concrete settings — a town next to the Yangtze, a small county town, a small city — there are few specific characteristics which mark out these places; they are representative of a large part of China. Though the emotions of the characters in the story are universal, their circumstances are grimly Chinese. References to famines, housing problems, the difficulties of job transfers, and particularly the interference of the "leadership" in the private life of individuals all remind readers of the external forces which are at play. Illicit love affairs are not condoned, and even irreproachable ones have to be kept under cover: before the hero and his wife are married, they have to leave their dormitory separately in order to take a walk together in the wood despite the fact that the dormitory is almost empty. Whatever the setting of the story, a tragic conclusion is perhaps inevitable, but the setting of China during the Cultural Revolution gives the story an added sense of grimness and suffocation.

Although the "Three Loves" deal with the same theme — relationships between men and women — Wang Anyi's treatment of this theme is progressive rather than static. On the one hand we can look at the three stories as a progression from anti-romanticism (in *Love on a Barren Mountain*) to irony (in *Love in a Beautiful Valley*); of course the fact that a story is anti-romantic shows that the author is conscious of its romantic potentiality. On the other hand we can see them as a progression in the author's women-centred attitude: in *Love on a Barren Mountain* the heroine seeks ultimate fulfilment of her love through a double suicide; in *Love in a Small Town* the heroine, after her baptism of fire, is cleansed of all physical desires and turns the consequences of her love affair (bringing up two illegitimate children) into a sublimated experience; in *Love in a Beautiful Valley* the hero exists entirely as a figment of the heroine's emotional experience: the love affair might or might not have taken place, but what matters is not what has actually happened, but what has happened in the heroine's mind. In *Love in a Beautiful Valley*, in which the physical existence of the hero becomes irrelevant, Wang Anyi has perhaps achieved the ultimate in her women-centred love stories.

If Wang Anyi's perception of the relationship between men and women in love is fundamental to *Love on a Barren Mountain*, so, too, are her keen powers of observation and insight. The story has a rich array of details covering physical sensations such as hunger, fashion trends during and after the Cultural Revolution, and in particular the subtle ebb and flow of a young woman's emotions during courtship. Wang Anyi's perfect sense of rhythm and timing is perhaps most apparent in the scene in which the sons of cadres try to make conversation with the heroine in the sweet shop. Since the heroine refuses to talk to any of them there is no conversation, but the effect of her humming a song is to make the whole scene highly aural; it is also highly cinematic. It shows us another side of the author: light-hearted and humorous.

But what is most remarkable about Wang Anyi's prose is her ability to evoke surreal feelings through detailed realistic descriptions. In both *Love in a Small Town* and *Love on a Barren Mountain* there is one scene which transcends the ordinary and leaves an indelible memory in the mind of the reader. In the former story it is the dance rehearsal, symbolic of the physical consummation of the love affair between the hero and the heroine; in the latter it is

Introduction

the fire which destroys the big house built by the hero's grandfather. It is not a fire but a dance, a symphony, a celebration of destruction, helplessness and liberation. In a brief moment of brilliance the house is consumed. One is tempted to draw a parallel between this and the suicide at the end of the story, but that is perhaps beside the point. Rather, the burning house, with its whirling ashes and dancing flames, serves to convince us of the sheer technical brilliance of Wang Anyi as a writer.

This translation is based on the Hong Kong South China Press edition (1988), which includes all three stories in the "Three Loves" under the collective title *Love on a Barren Mountain*. I first started translating this story in September 1988, which makes it the most time-consuming project I have undertaken to date. I am grateful to Chu Chiyu, Janice Wickeri, Duncan Hewitt, and particularly to D.E. Pollard, for their help and suggestions. I hope readers will enjoy reading the book as much as I did translating it.

Eva Hung
Chinese University of Hong Kong
October 1990

CHAPTER ONE

I

In those days anyone who could play a tune like "Xinjiang Spring" would be admitted to the violin stream of the Central Conservatory.

II

A frail, slim young man with a huge hold-all slung across his shoulder followed his elder brother, who had left home as a youth, to Shanghai. He left behind him a big, gloomy house.

The afternoon sun was hurting his eyes — eyes that had been so accustomed to the dark that they glowed in the dark like a cat's, while in bright light they looked dim and muddled. His face was pale, and on it the sun had left uneven patches; even the flush looked sickly.

His tall, well-built brother walked straight ahead, and the crowd seemed to make way for him of its own accord. But he was forever colliding with other people and he never emerged from the collision the winner, but was always pushed to one side. So it was that he could not walk in a straight line. His brother turned back but could not see him, and when he found him he took him by the hand. His slim fingers were clasped in his brother's broad, warm palm, and only now did he feel secure. He looked at his brother with gratitude, feeling that there was so much he owed him, but he was too shy to say a word. With his hand clasped in the warmth of his brother's palm, he felt both happy and embarrassed; his hand had sweated a little.

His elder brother pressed his fingers gently — slim, long but strong fingers with fleshy fingertips and nails that had been cut close. "Good hands for the violin," he thought, and gave that hand a tight squeeze. That hand, out of humility and shyness, remained still. He could not but be moved. He remembered the gloomy house in their home town, where their grandfather always sat in the middle of the main hall, and how on both sides of his hooked nose his eyes darted out piercing flashes of light. In the open courtyard surrounded by high walls his father drifted by noiselessly like the wind. His mother was busy in all the darkest corners, her back bent with labour. A brood of younger brothers and sisters, sometimes quiet, sometimes noisy, all had eyes like cats, shiny at night and dim in the day ....

"Tired?" He turned to ask his younger brother; his voice was loud, cutting out the humdrum chatter around them.

"No," he answered softly, with a slight country accent that skimmed past like a musical note.

His brother smiled: "If you're tired, just tell me."

"I will," he answered with his eyes downcast. His feet, clad in black canvas shoes, were trying laboriously to keep pace with his sturdy brother.

They got on the tram. It left the station and clattered merrily along its rails. He and his elder brother were seated separately, divided by the aisle. Later the seat next to his brother was vacant, and he longed to move over there and sit with him but he could not make up his mind. He was afraid that before he got there the tram would start again and he would lose his balance and fall down. Besides, he was also very shy. When his brother left home he was barely three years old. He only knew that Brother had gone first to

Shanghai to study fine arts, and then for some reason went on to northern Suzhou and joined first the New Fourth Army and then the Xin'an performance troupe. Later he went back to Shanghai where he became a violinist. And after that Brother came home; he stayed for just three days and took him along when he left. To him Brother was like a stranger and yet there was a blood-tie between them and he loved him from the bottom of his heart. He wanted to be close to him, and yet he was not bold enough to show it. He dared not look at Brother, but instead looked over his shoulders at the scene outside. There were so many people and so many things: he was dazzled, and his eyes could not focus on anything concrete. All the people and things converged into a colourful stream which flowed past under his eyes. The sunlight was blinding. Though only one night and one morning had passed, it seemed that the gloomy house and all that was in it belonged to another life. He recalled vaguely and yet distinctly, as if from a past life, his grandfather's aquiline nose that always looked as though it was about to peck at something. It separated two eyes which moved independently of each other and could not maintain friendly relations. He saw his mother. Mother hung a small cloth purse attached to a string around his neck and there were five *yuan* inside. Her hand touched his sharp ribs; his ribs touched her hand. He could never brush away that contact.

"We're getting off." Brother's voice penetrated the hum of the other voices; it made him shiver.

He stood behind Brother's wall-like back and waited for the tram to stop. He was a little nervous, fearing that he might not be able to jump off before the door closed again. He watched the door and gripped the strap of the hold-all he was carrying across his shoulder; the strap was pressing against the exact place where Mother had touched him.

The door closed behind him. He had not even caught his breath when Brother started marching forward again. No one could obstruct Brother, but people were forever knocking against him. When he saw someone walking straight towards him his bearing would show that he was going to give way, and so the other person felt he had every right to push him aside. Ducking all the time and walking in a crooked line, he was afraid that he would lose sight of Brother. Brother was walking in front, as eye-catching as ever; even people who were as tall as him somehow looked shorter. Brother was waiting at the entrance to an alley and looking in his direction with agitation and concern. He felt tears welling up inside him.

III

There was a quiet, shallow bay on the coast of the Yellow Sea, which was connected with the East Sea, and by the bay there was a town. The town had a mountain as a backdrop and looked out to the sea, and though the mountain was neither very tall nor very big, there were many stories associated with it. The townsfolk all knew that this mountain was the home of the Monkey King in *The Journey to the West*. There was this legend circulating in town: One year, a scholar went to the capital to take the imperial examination but failed. On his way home he felt that he could not face up to his family and relatives, and decided to live on this mountain as a recluse. He was a singularly ugly man with a face scarred by small-pox, and was thus ashamed to be seen. Day after day he stayed on the mountain where he ate wild fruits and drank from the mountain streams. For entertainment he carved a chess board on a slab of stone and played chess with himself, but this did not make time pass any more quickly and he was still bored. His imagination began to run wild, and he wrote that novel unique in the history of Chinese literature — *The Journey to the West*. The story was written on paper and has therefore travelled far and wide with the wind, but the mountain has its roots in the ground and could not budge an inch.

That was why most people thought that the Mountain of Fruits and Flowers and the Cave of the Water Curtain were all writer's inventions. No one knew that there was indeed such a mountain left untouched in a little dent in the Yellow Sea coastline, where only tiny boats could enter. To travel by train from there you had to go to Xuzhou first before you could go on to the rest of the country. Few people left the town, and few people came in. The townsfolk lived their lives between the mountain and the sea and the population boomed because of the high birth-rate and low death-rate. Their boys and girls were all as pretty as flowers. One drawback, however, was that their clothes were never in fashion. They just copied the way people from Xuzhou dressed, and decked themselves out in all the wrong ways.

Some years earlier a little girl had been born in Golden Corn Lane in the east of the city. She cried in a loud, clear voice as if she were singing. Her little face was like a pink cloud; everyone said that they had rarely seen such a beautiful baby. But they also said that given such a place and such a mother, it was little wonder that the woman should have such a coquettish daughter.

The little girl just kept on crying as if she were singing.

IV

Three hundred *li* west of the real-life Mountain of Fruit and Flowers there was a small, brand new city, so small that it could only be rated a town, but still, it had county status, and it was a new county. There were a large number of people from other provinces, and they all spoke standard Chinese with different accents, so much so that people's speech here resembled dialects all over China. The town was actually close to the Yellow Sea, and yet it was named Qinghai, the same as Qinghai province in north-western China. Not only was this name confusing, it did not even reflect the truth.

There was a small theatrical troupe in town which specialized in Henan operas. It received no state subsidy and all the members lived in a small house with a courtyard. It was here that they played their musical instruments and practised singing; it was also here that they went about their daily routines such as eating, drinking, and relieving themselves.

To the north of the small house there was a wood with a variety of trees. Day in and day out, an *erhu*[1] was played in the wood; its song was like weeping.

V

His elder brother gave him an hour-long lesson in music theory, sight-reading and aural-training every day. He was good at theory. Whatever he was told he would remember, and he could recite the strings of Latin terms by heart. This took his brother by surprise. His hearing was similarly sharp. After two months' practice no musical chord could escape him. Even when he broke a bowl he could give you the pitch it made on the piano. But he would not open his mouth to sing. His face was red and contorted, and tears welled up in his eyes, but no sound came from his mouth. His sister-in-law, who had been a mezzo-soprano, accompanied him on the piano and gently coaxed him to relax. But this made him even more nervous. His brother became angry, told him that if he failed to get into the Conservatory's secondary school he would have to go home. He bent his head and his slim fingers clutched together, but before they formed a fist they relaxed and hung limply. His fingertips turned red and then pale. After that he sang, but only very softly, and you had to hold your breath to hear him. His voice

---

[1] A Chinese string instrument similar to the violin, the *erhu* has two strings and is placed upright on the musician's knee.

was slightly hoarse, but he never sang out of tune, and if you listened for a long time you'd lose yourself in it.

Then he was enrolled at the Conservatory's secondary school as a cello major. His teacher was a woman, but she had hands like a man's, and a voice like a man's. Compared with her he was much more like a woman. She pushed him onto a chair and slapped him in the small of the back to make him sit straight. He did, but her hands stayed pressed against his back, giving out a penetrating warmth. He sat straight, not daring to move, but in his heart he was quite pleased — pleased that she was a woman and yet did not look like a woman. She handed him the cello; it leaned against his knees. The cello slid down until it fell to the floor, but she forbade him to hold onto it with his hands or with his knees. He was only allowed to rest the fingers of his left hand lightly against the cello's neck and the back of the fingerboard. She had told him before where the neck of the cello was. His thumb was pushed gently against the cello's neck, and his index finger, middle finger, third finger and little finger rested lightly on the fingerboard. The cello slid down, and there was nothing he could do about it. But then came the second day, and the third, and the fourth, the cello did not slide down anymore. There was nothing to stop it from sliding; everything was just as before. But it did not slide down anymore; it rested naturally against him. The bow slid over the strings.

His strings sounded. All the teachers and students said that the sound from his cello had a particularly rich quality, and they all watched him play and studied the angle his bow was placed against the strings and the force he used. He himself was puzzled. To him it was only natural, like the blowing wind and the flowing water. He loved playing; even playing the basic notes without fingering was fun. He loved every sound that came from the strings; it was as if the cello was talking to him. And when he played, it seemed that he was talking to his cello. For each and every question he asked there was a corresponding reply; it never failed. This was perhaps all there was to his secret. Just as his classmates were puzzled by him, so he was puzzled by them: How could they play for hours without saying anything, and without getting any reply? When he passed by his classmates' practice rooms, he would knit his brows, impatient with the dull and empty notes. His teacher was proud of him; so was his brother.

He went to his elder brother's place every Sunday morning. His sister-in-law had given birth to a pretty baby boy; they all said that it looked like him when he was small. He saved up the meal money his brother gave him and bought a rattle which he hung on his nephew's cradle. When the cradle gently rocked, the rattle sang a rasping tune.

He loved his brother and sister-in-law from the bottom of his heart, and he loved this little nephew whom they all said looked like him, but he did not know how to express his feelings. He was extremely tense whenever he was in his brother's place: even when his stomach was rumbling from hunger, the minute he sat down at table for lunch, he lost his appetite. He stared at all the good food his sister-in-law piled on his dish and actually felt sick. But as soon as the table was cleared his stomach started rumbling again.

He would have loved to help his sister-in-law with the housework, but he dared not. He locked himself up in the bathroom for a long time and stared at those nappies soaking in the basin: Should he wash them or not? He really wanted to. What a pleasure it would be to wash with his own hands the nappies that smelled of milk! But he was afraid that the nanny who looked after the new mother would fight over this work with him. He'd never have won, and the thought of such a scene embarrassed him. But he really wanted to wash them, to do something, however little, to repay his brother and his family for their kindness. The struggle was almost painful. If no one had knocked on the door to hurry him, his misery would probably never have ended.

He felt so awkward in his beloved brother's house that there was nothing he could do, and he left right after lunch every time, no matter how hard they pressed him to stay. He ran like a fugitive out of the lane where his brother lived and felt more relaxed, but also deeply sorry. The happiness that he had longed for for a whole week was finished; the next round of longing had begun. Why was it that the happiness he so desperately craved turned into an unbearable burden? He did not know; he only felt depressed. And in the depth of his depression he became homesick. Home was such a dark, hollow mansion that every time he thought about it, his eyes were filled with darkness. From the depths of the darkness a pair of sharp, falcon eyes emerged, piercing the darkness and advancing towards him. He could not help shivering. At such moments he felt completely alone, with no one to turn to. His heart was filled with love for his family and yet it could not find a resting place. He spent the holiday afternoon wandering up and down the busy Huaihai Road. He desperately wanted to go back to school and practise the cello, but he could not stand the solitude of school during a holiday. There would be no one except the old care-taker at the school entrance who would surely ask: "Why have you come back so early?" And he would have nothing to say in reply.

The smell of cream cakes and cosmetics wafted along Huaihai Road; the fragrance aroused his appetite. A little girl holding a candy stick was heading towards him. She looked as noble and serene as a princess, and he moved aside to let her pass. The sky in this city was so blue that it looked austere, and the sun so bright that it seemed threatening. He had lost the protection of the darkness that he was used to since childhood, and he felt like a small boat adrift on the open sea, always worrying that he would sink. Though he was not going anywhere, he walked very fast, as if he was chasing something or running away from something. After he had walked down several streets he thought it was time to turn back, but he was afraid that if he reversed directions abruptly he would arouse other people's suspicion, so he pretended to have suddenly thought of something and turned back, all the while scared that people would see through his pretence. He walked back and forth, which made him physically exhausted, but mentally he was more tense than ever.

At last the sky darkened; the pedestrians became fewer, but the street lamps had not yet been lit. Gradually he became calm and his pace slowed down; he was more relaxed. Dusk enveloped him like a warm curtain, reassuring and comforting him. It was time to go back to school. At this time the school would be very lively, with the sound of music intertwining with the students' clamour. But he did not want to go back now. He loved the dark streets. The faces of the pedestrians could not be distinguished; everyone was hurrying home and he was the only one at leisure. As dusk gathered he felt intoxicated. Forgetting everything, he just ambled on.

Then all the lights were suddenly turned on — fluorescent lights in the shop windows, street lamps amid the tree leaves, neon lights on the shop signs — all turned on at the same moment. The lights turned night into day; this was a city which did not sleep. He was stunned by this brightness that had come so suddenly. He quickened his pace and ran towards the school.

He ran straight into the practice room; only then did he feel reassured. His cello was leaning against the chair, its surface shimmering beautifully under the fluorescent light.

VI

On the bank of the Yangtze there was a medium size city. At the southern end of the city there was a dark, grand mansion. In the mansion there sat an old man, motionless like a buddha. He had an aquiline nose and piercing, falcon eyes. In his time he had been employed in almost every occupation you could name, and finally he started a timber company. Later the timber company was turned into a state-private joint venture.[2] Before this change took place he only had time to build one mansion, using the best timber there was. And then he was left with nothing except this timber mansion and numerous grand-children. Every day, in the morning and in the evening, he ordered his daughter-in-law to gather all his grand-children in front of him, and he looked at them like a general inspecting his army, but he never said anything and never allowed the others to say anything. After a very long time, he merely moved his shiny eyeball, and his daughter-in-law waved her hand at the children. In a second, silently, like ghosts, they were all gone.

He held in his hand a walking stick with a carved dragon head. Besides stumping the floor he also beat people with it. He never beat his son — the one who was to become head of the family after him could not afford to lose his dignity. Instead he beat his daughter-in-law as an example to his grand-children and as a silent warning to his son: beating your wife is the same as beating you; you may be above the rest but you are still under my command.

His daughter-in-law married into the family at the age of sixteen. She loved listening to the sirens from the boats, the boats that came from a far, far away place, and travelled to a far, far away place. She waited silently, waiting for the children to grow up so that she could send them to a far off land. She had seen off her eldest, and then the second child. The eldest got married and made a career for himself, but the second was lost; he died of typhus. Now she had seen off her third child. The eldest came back to take her third child away by the hand. They travelled by train, but somehow she always felt that they had gone by boat from the pier at the river bank. It seemed that only the Yangtze, flowing like a piece of white silk, could carry someone away.

The siren could be heard all over town.

---

[2] In the early 1950s the communist government turned all private companies into joint ventures with the state. Shortly afterwards everything was nationalized.

VII

After the massive scale steel production, after the massive "sputnik launching",[3] after the masses were ordered to eat in brigade canteens — all exciting heady days — the famine came.[4]

Tens of thousands starved to death during the famine. Everyone had to tighten his belt and go hungry, but there was one old man with falcon eyes who refused to accept this endurance test prescribed by heaven. He had to have his three meals every day, and his snacks as well. The responsibility of providing for him fell onto his grandchildren; his grandchildren finally had a chance of repaying him for his care and protection.

Brother had to send more than double the usual amount of money home, and could only afford to give him the bare minimum for his meals. He was growing up then, and his bones stuck out from his almost transparent skin. All his shirts and pants had shrunk by a couple of inches, exposing his thin wrists and ankles. He was hungry all the time, day and night, and the hunger was like a fire burning inside him. In his mind there was only one word — hunger. It was only when he was practising at his cello that he could briefly forget about his hunger. Yet within a few minutes it attacked him in another form. A cold sweat broke out on his forehead, his fingers shook, his heartbeat quickened, and he could not press the strings down flat. The strings almost cut his fingers, but he still failed to touch the fingerboard. He tried in vain, and was soon exhausted.

Brother told him to come back for a meal every Sunday. An

---

[3] This was a slogan which referred to achieving new records in agriculture and industry.

[4] This refers to the Great Leap Forward Campaign of 1958. Mao Zedong ordered everyone in the country, farmers, soldiers, students and housewives alike, to join in the production of steel. As a result agricultural production was neglected and the country suffered from famine in 1958-60.

exact amount of rice was measured and put into two containers which were then steamed. When it was done his sister-in-law carefully divided the rice in each container into two equal halves, one half for each person. He and his brother shared one, and his nephew and his sister-in-law shared the other. His nephew was two years old, but he had a bigger appetite than any grown man. Once he actually drank a whole saucepanful of noodle soup. This was the best meal he had had for a whole week, but it only served to stir up his appetite. He walked out of his brother's house onto Huaihai Road. That fragrant smell wafting on the wind hit him in the face. He could not control his craving for food, and yet he *had* to control it somehow. He walked on, surrounded by the scent of fresh cream, holding back his tears. So great was his anguish that he wanted to run his head against a lamp post and kill himself. But the lamp post moved, and as he drew near it suddenly grew to a tremendous height. He drew back in a hurry.

In the dormitory his schoolmates were cursing, sighing or even crying, complaining about the different sensations of hunger and recalling the delicacies they had had in the past, hoping that this insubstantial talk would satisfy their hunger. He could not stand listening to any of this. He buried his head in his quilt and stuck his fingers in his ears, trying hard not to hear, trying hard to fall asleep. But a battle seemed to be going on inside his stomach. His intestines twisted painfully; his stomach suddenly opened out into an empty hole, ready to swallow anything and everything. Then just as suddenly it shrank into a small compact lump stuck in his chest. For some reason he recalled that as a child he had watched his mother wash the fatty guts of pigs: a chopstick was inserted at one end of a very long intestine, and the whole thing was pulled inside out. Meanwhile his hearing had become incredibly sharp. He could hear every single word of his schoolmates' complaints which aroused in him unlimited desire. Saliva welled up in his mouth, and he swallowed hard, swallowing until he felt sick. He was infuriated.

He hated them for shouting so loudly about hunger; he hated them for recalling the taste of good food. The shouting and the remembrance were in fact a means of venting their feelings, an escape. It was like people crying loudly when they are beaten. Besides, when everyone shouted together, it was also a kind of consolation: I'm not the only one who's hungry; you're hungry too, and so is he, and so is everybody. At the thought of this everyone calmed down. But he did not understand. He was fighting against hunger on his own and so it was even tougher for him. He ground his teeth, held his breath, trying hard to suppress his hunger. But it gnawed at him with added cruelty.

Once, in his brother's place, his brother was studying a score, his sister-in-law was steaming the rice, and his nephew was playing with building blocks on a small round table. The little boy was piling up building blocks and chewing at a biscuit with great relish. There was another biscuit on the table; it also belonged to his nephew. It was a rough, black biscuit shaped like a toy car, with curves crudely tracing out two fat wheels and the body. He could not take his eyes off it, and then his hand reached out for the biscuit and he put in into his mouth without any attempt at concealment. The fragrance of the biscuit filled his whole body, but in a brief second it disappeared; there was just too little of it. Only now did he panic, his face turning white in a flash. He stood up and walked out. His brother and sister-in-law called after him, but he did not even turn his head, just said that he had some business to attend to and walked out of the house. He went as far as the next lane and hid behind an iron gate, and he started crying. He was so ashamed of himself that he wanted to dig a hole and hide. He felt that from now on there would be a black mark in his life. And yet he could not understand what had happened just now. It was not what he had wanted to do; it was not like him at all. But the series of moves from the stretching out of his hand to putting the biscuit into his mouth was engraved on his memory and could never be erased. He thought that he had become a dirty, low person, like a thief. What was more, this wrong could not be righted because time would not reverse its course. He cried bitterly, shedding the tears that he had held back for days: tears of hunger, anger, home-sickness and loneliness. People going in and out of the lane saw him crying, but did not pay much attention. No one asked him why he was crying, and he was left alone to cry to his heart's content.

When he returned to school he used up the whole day's meal coupons to buy himself one single meal. As his lips touched the steaming congee, a feeling of bliss rose from the soles of his feet, and he shivered. He forgot about that pain and immersed himself in the joy of eating. But after he had finished the meal he had an unaccountable feeling of total defeat. He was so depressed that he did not know what to do, and he did not know what he was depressed about. Hunger, like lust, comes in several stages: craving is followed by joy, and joy is followed by a sense of defeat. But he did not understand this; he felt utterly despondent. At night, lying in bed, he brooded endlessly that he was no longer a clean person. He became nostalgic: the past was so beautiful; even hunger was pure then. But it was all over, from now on he was a sinner and he would have to shoulder the burden of his sin for the rest of his life. To him life was too long; he would never see the end of his days.

This was like a hole in a dam; the strength and tension he had mustered to help fight the hunger began to relax. Hunger became more and more invincible. One day he picked up a few pieces of scrap metal and sold them at a junk shop for a few cents which he spent on two small steamed buns. The buns were made of a special, transparent flour the texture of which, as he chewed, seemed almost like meat. The lard melted, and the sweet taste penetrated his whole body. After he had finished the buns, the blissful feeling receded at once, and was replaced by a sense of deep regret. He swore that he would never stoop so low again, swore that he would put the whole incident behind him and be a nice, clean boy again. He hid in a deserted place and cried, slapping his mouth and biting his own tongue, feeling that he would never change, feeling absolutely hopeless. But the flames of hunger rose again and again uncontrollably. Ever since that incident he was unable to resist any attack of hunger. At such times he forgot about shame; he searched the corridors, the playground, the classrooms for anything that could be exchanged for money. The second time he took a pack of electric wires out of the school, his nervous look attracted the attention of the old caretaker, who called at him to stop. A couple of questions from the old man made him confess everything.

He felt that the sky was falling straight onto his head, pushing him down into the ground. The ground was bottomless, and he just kept falling.

His brother was reading a score in front of the piano; his sister-in-law was measuring out rice for steaming; his nephew was piling up building blocks.

VIII

In the east of the city the little girl from Golden Corn Lane could talk now, and as soon as she had learned to talk she could sing little tunes. She had a clever tongue, and she pronounced every single word of the lyrics clearly:

The fine tresses on my head oh who's ruffling them up?
The ear-rings I'm wearing oh why is there only one left?
The powder on my face oh why is it wet?
The rouge on my lips oh who will come and taste it?

When the adults heard her they all laughed: "Where did she learn that little fairground song? Got it off to a tee, didn't she?" But after they laughed they made faces: She is singing a saucy song at such a young age, and singing it so coquettishly, who else would have a daughter like that?

The little girl did not hear any of this; she thought that everyone was praising her, that everyone liked her, and so she devoted her attention to making herself pretty. Young though she was, she knew how to choose the embroidery patterns for her shoes. She chose nothing but pink flowers, flowers so delicate that it seemed the wind could blow them away. When she had made her decision she urged her mother to start embroidering at once, and when it was done she would wear her new shoes outside to show them off. She did not skip or hop about like other children; she took one step at a time, turning her feet out ever so slightly and walking along a perfect straight line, like a knowing adult. All the children gathered around to look at her new shoes, but she faked impatience. She crossed her hands behind her and, leaning against the wall, looked at the orchids hanging in front of some household.

An "uncle" was approaching from the head of Pebble Lane, carrying fruit and wine. She recognized him from afar and was so excited that her face flushed, but she pretended not to see him. When he came right in front of her, she pretended to be angry, unhappy. When the uncle called her name, she did not answer; when he told her to come home with him, she went, seemingly unwilling, but in fact her heart was thumping with excitement. She had many "uncles", and every time they came they were never empty-handed. They brought goodies for her mother and for her too: crocheted flowers, satin ribbons, red jackets, and dolls with eyes that could move. She wanted to jump up and down for joy, but her mother eyed her angrily and scolded her for being cheap. She watched her mother, who always had a languid look. Even when the uncles gave her presents it did not please her; she told them off. But when the uncles were gone, Mother would place all the gifts in front of her and inspect them one by one, smiling. When no uncle came for a long time, Mother pulled a long face and took her anger out on the little girl, knocking her about as if she was deranged; she did not recover until the uncles came again. Gradually she learned:

The uncles' coming was a happy event, and yet she was not to show her happiness; not only was she not to show it, she had to pretend that she was not pleased because that was the classy way to behave.

The uncle this time brought her a pair of pink elasticated trousers from Shanghai which could be stretched to any length or width. After she had taken a look at the gift she relaxed, took a handful of melon seeds and went outside. Her little mouth cracked the melon seeds with great skill. In went one whole melon seed, and out came two neatly divided halves which fell here and there on the pebbled street. Her tiny teeth made a clear sound every time a melon seed was cracked open. The children looked at her from afar, not daring to go near her again because the grown-ups had forbidden them to do so. She did not mind any of this, just kept on eating her melon seeds that made clear noises as they cracked, like a song.

IX

300 *li* west of the town, in the little wood, the *erhu* was singing as if it were weeping.

X

It was only about two hours ago that the siren had sounded at the pier. His mother never expected that her third child would walk in just like that. The face which had been pale before was now the colour of cabbages; there were black circles around his eyes; he had grown taller but thinner, so much so that it seemed a breeze could blow him over. The huge hold-all he was carrying almost crushed his thin shoulder blades. At the sight of his mother his eyes turned red. He opened his mouth to speak several times without success.

Before his return his brother had taught him what to say: there was not enough food in Shanghai and the government had told the people to return to their homes in the country. His mother had too much to worry about already, and besides she cared a lot about appearances, that was why his brother warned him not to say that he had been expelled from school. But when he stood in front of his mother, he could not say a word. Seeing him like this, his mother seemed to hear a loud explosion in her head. Although she did not know about anything, it also seemed that she understood everything. She did not question him, just said: "Go and wash yourself."

He seemed to have been granted an amnesty. Obediently he put his things to one side, filled a basin with water and washed his face. His mother got on with sorting out some greens.

After he had washed, he opened his hold-all and took out two boxes of cakes: "From Brother, one for Grandpa, and one for you."

His mother took a glance at the boxes and said, "Your brother is again spending money needlessly." She did not say anything else.

The home-coming ceremony had been simple and smooth; he was back home again. He had been away for two years and the house looked even darker and more gloomy now. He spent all his days in a room at the back of the house, reading. There was a toon tree in the courtyard that was so tall it seemed to reach the clouds, and it blocked the light from the windows. Trying his best to catch the light that shone through the gaps in the foliage, he finished one thick book after another — *The Story of the Monk Ji Gong*, *The Journey to the West*, and *The Story of the Stone*. All day, except when presenting himself for three meals and the two summonses by his grandfather, he stayed in the back room, lying on a bamboo couch reading, or thinking. In fact he had little to think about, he just lay there, thinking about nothing. A sound flowed by his ears, the sound of the cello. In his mind there was always this exercise tune for the cello; the tune went up the scale and then down again, like climbing up and down a staircase. It progressed circuitously, two steps forward, one step back. When it reached the top it moved downward again, still taking two steps forward and one step back, still circuitously, never ceasing, never ending. Whatever he was doing, whether eating, sleeping, reading or being inspected by his grandfather, the tune kept on repeating itself. He longed fervently to play again, but he was too ashamed of himself to think about it; he thought he had no right to think about it anymore. Besides, memories of the cello were associated with the pain of shame and the degradation of sin. Or rather it was the pain of shame and the degradation of sin which were associated with memories of the cello. He wished that none of this had taken place, that it was all a senseless dream. Only by pretending that none of this had ever happened could he live peacefully, day by day.

Yet all this had happened. The thought that it had not happened was a dream. He could only dream about this peacefully in the back room, under the shade of the toon tree. The minute he walked out of the house and into the street, sunlight rained on him, so brilliant that he could not open his eyes, and the boats at the pier sounded their sirens — a long blast followed by a short one — and then a few acquaintances came up to say hello, and he woke up from his dream. That was why he needed the darkness more than ever before. He needed the protection of this darkness which he hated. He could not go out into the streets even if it was just to buy some matches or soy sauce, he just could not do it.

When his grandfather summoned the grandchildren he turned specifically to him and asked, "Are you deep in meditation? Are you reading the sutras? After spending two years in grand Shanghai you have become dignified and unfathomable, haven't you?" And then his grandfather smiled darkly. He could feel his mother's eyes on him, he could feel that she was worried, but he remained silent, his head bent. He had spent two years in Shanghai; nothing about him had changed except that he no longer thought much of his grandfather, which surprised him. Now he showed respect and fear for his grandfather out of consideration for his mother and from habit. He had been bold enough to imagine that if his awesome Grandpa were placed in a crowd in Huaihai Road, he would surely look insignificant. At the same time as he recognized the insignificance of his grandfather, he recognized his own insignificance, and felt at a loss, not knowing why he had come into this world, not knowing what he had come here for. In the dark room, in the flickering light that filtered through the gaps in the foliage, he felt empty, and sadness filled his heart. He thought that he was insignificant, but actually he was thinking too much of himself. Sheltered by the darkness, he magnified his feelings of shame, degradation, injustice and sadness freely and wilfully.

The sound of the cello was flowing by his ears, always present, singing the same tune. At the lower end of the scale the sound was rich and deep, at the upper end it was powerful and agitated; it mingled with the siren from the pier. The sound disturbed him; he could not even dream in peace.

On this day he heard the sound of his grandfather's walking stick falling on his mother's back. He felt it had to be his fault and he buried his head in his pillow crying woefully. His tears flowed uncontrollably, like a flood which had broken through a dam. Despair and hopelessness filled his heart. The world was peopled by the innocent and unfortunate; where could one find the smallest happiness? He cried until blood almost came out of his eyes, until he could cry no more, and then he gradually stopped. He lay on the bamboo couch, completely enervated, but at heart he felt calm and pure; he was almost beginning to be happy. The toon tree brushed against the window, sweeping tiny threads of the blood-red evening sunlight into the room. His legs and arms were limp, but his heart was crystal clear; it was as if the tears had washed all the impurities away.

After all he was only seventeen. No matter how weak he was, he was also full of a fresh vitality. The sense of gloom was temporary; there was plenty of hope. Before he used up this hope drop by drop he still had a long way to go, many pleasures to enjoy, and a lot of pain to bear.

The siren at the pier sounded faintly. It was like a call to mystery.

XI

In the town next to the bay by the Yellow Sea, the girl from Golden Corn Lane had started school. She had cut out the material for the school bag herself, and her mother had embroidered a pair of playful mandarin ducks on it. The ducks looked so real that if you had blown some air into them they would probably have come alive. The girl was wearing pink elasticated socks, red woollen shoes and a pale yellow pant suit in a floral print. The little shirt had purple piping and the trousers had slightly flared bottoms; the outfit could not have been prettier. None of the girls in her class wanted to walk with her. They feared that they could not match up to her, that she would look even better in comparison. She could not care less. Her face was slightly lifted; her hair, the tips of which had been permed with heated tongs, was tied into two plaits with curly ends like hydrangea flowers which bounced against her small, round shoulders. Step by step, her feet tracing a straight line, she walked to school.

In the whole classroom there was not a single child as clever and good-looking as her. She sat bolt upright, and she talked clearly. The teacher was pleased with her the first time she saw her, and made her the class monitor, so every lesson when the teacher came in she called on the class to stand up, and at the end of the day she led the class out of school. She was exceptionally good at reading other people's minds, and whatever the teacher said she remembered. When the teacher said that the stick used for pointing at the blackboard was not handy, the minute she got home she persuaded an uncle to make a new one, bound one end with coloured cords, and gave it to the teacher. Nor did she say much when she presented her present, just that they had this bamboo stick at home and her mother bound it with coloured cords and told her to give it to teacher. One Sunday her teacher went to the hairdresser and had her hair permed. The next day, during class, the teacher blushed with embarrassment, and after class she said to her teacher, "You look like someone in the pictures with your hair permed. When I grow up I want a perm too."

She was the teacher's little darling. On National Day there was a school gala and every class had to participate. The teacher asked her class to volunteer, but all the pupils showed false modesty: though they wanted to volunteer they were embarrassed, afraid that others would say they were vainglorious. She was the only one who behaved naturally and raised her hand. When the teacher called her name, she walked up to the podium confidently, stood still, bowed, then folded her hands lightly in front of her chest and sang: "Beautiful Havana, my home is there." Her voice was crisp and clear, and she could reach any note, no matter how high. The teacher asked her to stay behind and choreographed some movements for her to go with the song. She went through it once and got it perfectly. But her little finger, like the tiny tip of a slim bamboo shoot, was always raised high. The teacher did not like it, but she could not tell why.

Hers was the most popular item in the gala. In the assembly hall the applause was earth-shaking. She bowed again and again, and then she walked down from the stage, unhurried and bolt upright. Pupils from all classes stood up to stare at her. She was delighted, but did not show it, and actually pretended to be impatient with them. She walked back to her own seat at a perfectly even pace, sat down squarely and lifted her face to look at the stage, as if she did not feel a thing.

XII

300 *li* to the west, in the little wood, there were moving shadows of people practising martial arts and the flickering of light reflected on swords and spears. Those engaged in vocal training sang out notes high and low, and the *erhu* was singing as if it were weeping.

XIII

In the streets and in schools the government was advocating the way of Xing Yanzi and Dong Jiageng.[5] He signed up. After a week his application was approved. In company with over a hundred youths with a red flower pinned on their shirts, he boarded a train and left. The train moved out of town into the open fields, and he felt at ease. He pulled the window half open and let the wind blow on his long hair. In the carriage the students were singing.

The farm he went to bordered on Anhui province on one side and Shandong province on the other. Its chief crop was originally wheat, but just now the fields were being converted into rice paddies. Everyone pulled up their trousers to work in the water-covered fields. Walking on the narrow ridges carrying basketfuls of

---

[5] These were "model students" of the early 1960s who volunteered to go to the countryside.

seedlings was like a circus performance. He did not try to spare himself but picked the hardest tasks. He fell down from the ridges more than once, covering himself in mud, unable to get back on his feet. The others all laughed and extended their hands to help him up and told him to go home and change. But he refused to go, just picked up his baskets and carried on. With his wet clothes clinging to him, he was soon shivering. Then his clothes were baked dry by the sun and the warmth of his body. It was a wonderful moment when he peeled the warm clothes away; every cranny of his body felt warm.

At night, when he lay in bed, all his joints ached and he could not move at all. The aching pleased him, and he was relaxed at heart. To get up the next morning was like torture, but he gritted his teeth and pushed himself up, put his feet on the ground to grope for his shoes, and when he finally located them, he stood up and walked out in long strides. He was even more heedless than the day before, and when he heard his bones crack, he felt happy. He bent under the heavy load he was carrying on his shoulder pole and stumbled along, in a zigzag, but he did not fall down. The locals all said that he was risking his life; they also said that he was a good, honest lad. He made his own meals, but it was almost unnecessary for him to cook anything, for all his neighbours on the farm gave him preserved vegetables — spiced beans, salty garlic, dried turnips. Any family that had prepared meat and fish dishes to feast their guests always asked him along. They were concerned that he was so thin and weak, and besides, it was an honour to have a student from the city in their company.

This was a brand new life. Everything from the past had receded, hidden in a shady corner of his memory. He was glad that he had made the right decision and he could not bear to think back on the days before he came here. To him this was like a rebirth. The accounts of the past had all been settled, and here life began anew.

His skin became tanned and he grew stronger. Although he remained taciturn he looked much more relaxed. He laboured in the day, and at night he either talked to the young people in the village about stories and happenings in the city, or he went to the neighbouring production brigades to visit school friends. When he walked back the moon was shining brightly in the sky, the water was flowing in the irrigation channels, wheat was growing quietly in the fields, and from afar some playful dogs were barking. He walked along the road which had turned snow-white under the moonlight; mist had penetrated the ground, and through his cloth shoes he could feel the earth's suppleness. He started humming, and did not realize what he was humming for quite a while: it was that exercise tune for the cello. Events from the past welled up in his mind. On this moonlit night, the shadows cast by past events seemed much paler, and he was aware only of a slight sorrow which suited his present peaceful frame of mind. Frogs were croaking in the fields, and he recalled the events of the past one by one. He had suddenly lost his sense of fear and shame about the past; he only felt a slight pain. The pain could not hurt him now, for he was much stronger than before. Now that he could cope with farm work easily and playfully, he even thought that he should do something else so that his life would not be wasted.

It so happened that a woman teacher in the primary school of their production brigade had left to join the army and he was asked to fill the vacancy. He taught Chinese, arithmetic, natural science and geography to fourth, fifth and sixth graders. Later on he discovered a forty-eight key bass concertina in the school, got hold of a few basic manuals, and actually succeeded in playing a few songs. So he gave music lessons to the whole school. Every night, after the marking was done, he sat in front of the school gate and played the concertina. It was the happiest time for him.

He had a special way of playing the concertina. He did not pull at the bellows with any deliberate effort; he let it move of its own accord. His right hand moved along the keyboard as if fondling it; each note came out soft and down-to-earth, never making a grand show. His left hand merely touched the bass studs, and there was never an unnecessary movement. The treble side was playing a melody as pure as if it had come from a flute, a melody that was lingering in the air, when the bass suddenly joined in. The playing gradually livened up, gathering natural momentum, and now the bass side introduced a light but powerful rhythm. When his emotion was at its height, when it was beyond control and could not reach any higher, there came a loud, shattering chord. And then suddenly the sound stopped. It was quiet all around, and then a tune that was weeping as well as pleading, sad as well as happy rose again from the ground.

He rested his head on the concertina, his eyes half-closed. He thought about nothing, just gave his mind completely over to the concertina. His fingers spoke to the keys, and the keys answered him. Deep into the night he suddenly looked up wide awake. From the position of the stars he knew it was very late; the sky was filled with stars which seemed to have surrounded him.

XIV

A mere slip of a girl, she already knew how to flirt with men. Her words were sharp but she had a sense of proportion. Everyone said that she was not the girl from Golden Corn Lane for nothing. She was the tops.

All around the bay by the Yellow Sea she was the only one who knew how to dress herself. She even looked down on the fashion styles from northern Xuzhou, and instead tried to learn from the films. One day she would tie her hair into two long plaits right at the back of her head so that they almost touched. The ends of the plaits were tied together with a red satin ribbon with a large bow which swung near her slender waist. That was fashionable. A couple of days later her hair style changed. The plaits were coiled up on either side of her head, like those of a lady's maid in the operas, with a small red comb clasped on the right side which made her look ever so cute. A couple of days later it changed again. Her hair was parted on one side and a red string was woven into her two plaits, one right above each shoulder, and she was wearing a fringe. This made her look like a country girl, but it gave her an air of freshness and innocence. People's eyes were not quick enough for the tricks she had. They all felt that she changed like quicksilver, that it was impossible to pin her looks down. She was like a siren who played tricks on men. And yet whichever way you looked at her, she was beautiful. The boys in her class called her names such as "big flirt" and "bourgeoise" in front of others, but behind each other's back they gave her little things like pencils decorated with patterns, transparent rulers and snow-white paper-pads.

She did not even lift her eyes to look at them: "Don't want them."

"Why not? It's good," said the boy.

"If it's good, keep it for yourself."

"It's for you."

"Don't want it." She did not lift her eyes.

The boy got angry: "All right, forget it!"

But then she turned to look at him, her pupils black and shiny, swimming in her deep-set eyes, smiling: "Angry?"

And so he could not very well be angry with her.

She learned all this from her mother. That was how her mother treated her uncles. A happy look was a precious thing, you had better not show it easily. And yet you could not be too harsh; you had to look happy at the right moment, or else it would be useless and worthless however precious the look was. The "right moment" was always in her mother's mind; she must judge it to the second. If she handled it right the men would all be her slaves. But if her anger turned real, the men would just turn and walk away and would not be ordered about. Her uncles were all her mother's slaves; her mother's every smile and sulk were all right on beat. She watched them and thought it was fun, so sometimes she wanted to have a go, to experiment. It worked! She was pleased.

For the spring picnic the teacher took them to the Mountain of Fruit and Flowers, and they climbed into the Cave of the Water Curtain. Everyone thought that the cave was too small and too plain, that it was not good enough to be the Monkey King's palace. She argued with them, claiming that the entrance to the cave was small because later generations had blocked it up, that inside it was huge and deep, and that shameless people were always coming here to do shameless things, that this was not only a violation of the sacred site but a damage to social morality. She learned all this from her uncles. The children were curious: What were the things that had to be done in the cave? they all asked. She jeered at their ignorance. Actually she herself was not any better informed. A little boy refused to believe her, kept arguing with her. She thought he was cute, so she said: Let's climb in together and knock on the wall of the cave. If it has been blocked up, then it will give a hollow sound, otherwise the sound will be solid.

So the two of them climbed in and knocked on the wall. Their little hands hit against the wall, and the sound they made was not even as loud as a slap on the face. Yet she said immediately, "Listen, it's a hollow sound." The little boy listened hard for a while, still confused and smiling foolishly, when all of a sudden the girl kissed him on the lips. For a moment it felt warm, and wet, and he did not understand what it meant, but the girl blushed deeply, hastened out of the cave and caught up with the others, her heart thumping, very happy.

The Mountain of Fruit and Flowers had neither fruit nor flowers. It was a deserted, barren mountain, with not a trace of men in sight.

XV

300 *li* to the west there was a small county town. It was right next to Jinan prefecture and yet it was ruled from Nanjing; it was close to the Yellow Sea but they call it Qinghai. What a joke!

In the town there was a little wood, and in the wood people were practising martial arts, singing and playing their musical instruments. The *erhu* was singing as if it were weeping.

XVI

At that time all the primary and middle schools and the universities closed down. It was the Cultural Revolution.

XVII

There was a letter from home: Grandpa had been taken away by the "revolutionaries" and there had been no news of him for seven days and nights; father was ill in bed; his younger brothers and sisters were all classified as members of the Five Black Categories[6] and were pilloried in school every day; there had been no news of his elder brother.... Could he come home for a visit? And if there were some beans or corn please bring a little with him. The letter was written by his fourth brother behind their mother's back. His mother was too proud to ask her own son for help.

He travelled by night to northern Xuzhou, carrying a sack of rice and wheat (his grain ration for six months) and walked

---

[6] The Five Bad Categories were landlords, rich peasants, counter-revolutionaries, rightists and bad elements.

effortlessly and rhythmically onto the railway platform. The train blew its horn and started, travelling southward in the morning mist. When he reached home it was already dark. His mother was taken aback; she almost could not recognize him, and when she did her face softened. Mother had aged; her fair skin was now dry and wrinkled, but she still dressed neatly. He put the sack down on the floor and greeted her: "Mum", but his voice was hoarse.

Mother just said, "Go and wash yourself." She did not ask questions, as if it was only right that he should be back. But he felt that his mother understood everything. Mother was extremely wise. Though she was frequently beaten by her father-in-law in front of her own children, she never lost her dignity. She was naturally dignified. She tried her best to put her children on the right path, but if they did wrong she never blamed them; she seemed to think that it was all unavoidable, all fated. Everyone in the family depended on her, including his father and grandfather. If it were not for her, how was his grandfather to give vent to his anger and show off his power? That would be a big problem.

Not until dinner time did he fully realize how poverty-stricken his family had become. The sack of grain he brought back was a life-saver. His grandfather had been dispatched home under escort two nights ago. He was as thin as a stick, but his eyes were burning, and his nose had never been as sharp and pointed as now; he looked evil. After he came back he had stayed in bed, refusing to get up, also refusing food and water. Mother tried to talk to him but he hit her on the back with his walking stick; Father pleaded with him on his knees, but he shut his eyes and pretended not to hear, pretended to be dead. And yet because the twice-daily summonses had been cancelled, the atmosphere at home was much more relaxed. His younger brothers and sisters had become much more lively, especially since his return from the countryside. But life was difficult for them. The monthly interest from the timber factory was withheld, and his father's salary was meagre. None of his brothers and sisters had a job; he had been out in the countryside and could not be counted on to help, and as for his brother in Shanghai, they did not even know whether he was alive. It was his fifth sister who, using the name of a good friend, got herself an odd job pasting match boxes. They did not have to go to school anymore, so the brothers and sisters sat around a square table every day and worked hard at making match boxes. As soon as he arrived home he joined in, and he quickly got the knack. With the dexterous fingers of a musician he caught up with his brothers and sisters in speed as well as quality.

Pasting match boxes was a boring job, but chatting was fun. Because of the fun, even the boring job became attractive. Every day their hands flew as they pasted the boxes together; it was mechanical work that did not require thinking, and as they worked they talked about all sorts of interesting things. The cruel struggles in society had shattered their peaceful daily life; it had also shattered the strict rules and regulations at home. Those difficult days often afforded the children some pleasure. They were young and unwilling to be suppressed. As they talked, they sometimes forgot themselves and laughed loudly, and their merry laughter was heard in the bedroom where their grandfather was lying. The laughter was contradictory to what was happening in the world. Grandfather hammered on the floor furiously with his walking stick. The phlegm that gurgled and blustered in his throat seemed to be roaring on his behalf. The children made faces and suppressed their laughter; instead of laughing they just snickered through their noses. But Grandfather's heavy breathing did not quieten for a long time. He had not eaten for six days and six nights. The body that was lying between the sheets seemed to have disappeared. From afar you could see only a high, aquiline nose and two exceptionally brilliant eyes.

Because they were young, it did not take too much to make them laugh. They frequently forgot themselves, forgot about the cruel things that were happening in this crazy world, forgot that in the bedroom in the west wing lay a weakened old man unwilling to accept his fate. As for him, back at the side of his mother and brothers and sisters after such a long absence, his heart was filled with love. Besides, at this point in his life he could see no future for himself, and this exempted him from exerting himself; he could now take a break. Life was difficult, but a burden was lifted from his heart. Their laughter drowned the angry hammering of the walking stick in the west wing bedroom. They no longer paid attention to their grandfather's existence. Then one day, the old man suddenly called out for their mother in an exceptionally loud and clear voice and said that he wanted a bowl of soup. She hurriedly made a bowl of egg soup in which she put laver, table salt and MSG, and brought it piping hot into the bedroom. He told her to leave it on one side and go out.

Two hours later, his fourth brother who was seated at the table facing west suddenly changed colour and stammered in the middle of a conversation. Everyone turned to look, and they all stood up automatically. Grandfather was standing unsteadily at the door of the west wing bedroom, both hands on his walking stick. The long gown he was wearing seemed to be hanging on a clothes-hanger; it fell straight to the ground. Having grown thin, he looked exceptionally tall, and his aquiline nose had an imposing dignity. His gaze was like a blade that cut across the top of their heads. Mother went across to him to offer him support, but he drove her away with his walking stick. He stood there for a while before he began to walk, very slowly, towards the main sitting room. Everyone made way for him in silence. He walked slowly along the wall, passing one room after another, then crossed the garden into the courtyard. Everyone followed him from afar, not understanding what he meant to do. He paced through every corner of the house, and then slowly he turned to go back to his bedroom. By now it was almost dusk.

That evening the sky darkened very rapidly. As soon as the sun had set, it was completely dark.

That night the sky was exceptionally dark. He could not even see his own fingers, and the shadows of the toon leaves completely disappeared. There was not even the dimmest light from the sky, which seemed to have been sealed off with a thick black curtain. He slept under that black curtain and felt its pressure on his eyes. Suddenly the curtain became light, pale, bright, and slowly it turned a bright red, like blood, it was burning and scary. He did not understand: why was he wrapped in this redness? Surrounding him were four red, fiery walls; even the sky was red. He struggled, trying to wake himself from this nightmare, but he was woken up by a shrill scream. It was his mother. He had never before heard her screaming so piercingly and in such great fear, but it *was* Mother screaming — "Fire!"

It was a fire. It started on the ground, climbed up the walls and enveloped the whole house. The whole house was in flames; the flames were rising up in joy and ardour. He sat up and rushed out of bed. At the same time he pushed his fourth brother, who was sleeping beside him, onto the floor and dragged him out of the room. The rotted door lintel was collapsing gracefully. He lost his reason and rushed towards it, but a pair of powerful arms held him back; it was Mother. Mother held Father by the hand; his young brothers and sisters clung together, like little chicks; the lintel collapsed gracefully in a trail of flames.

Mother gave him a push and he ran through the door. The rooms beyond the courtyard were also on fire.

"Father!" His father cried in a shrill and doleful voice. Grandfather's bedroom door was barred; the fire had turned the door panels almost transparent.

"Grandpa!" They shouted together. The fire hissed; that was the only response they had.

The fire was closing in on them. The beams of the house looked like fiery red piano keys overhead, ready to collapse at any minute. Mother hesitated no longer. She grabbed their father and herded everyone together. Finally they rushed out of the flames into the street. It was like rushing from a fiery pit into an ice house. The night was cold, and everyone in the family was wearing light clothing. The younger ones among his brothers and sisters only had their underpants on. They held onto each other, shivering, looking at the blazing house.

The house had never been so brilliant or so beautiful before. It was like a palace. At the moment of its funeral its customary darkness and gloom were completely dispelled. It seemed that the purpose of its entire existence was in this destruction, that it had lived through the gloomy decades just for this moment of brilliance. Against the dark blue sky, the flames traced out the outline of the house, surrounded by black ash fluttering around it, like ghosts singing a silent requiem.

"That's your grandpa's life-long work!" Father wept.

All of a sudden the whole house became transparent, like a crystal palace, and then it collapsed quietly. The flames lay on the ground, dancing silently. It began to drizzle, and bit by bit the fire was extinguished.

The whole family was drenched, and they had been shivering for so long that they were frozen. The neighbours opened their doors and pulled the grown-ups and the children into their houses for shelter, but none of them wanted to go in. They all stood in the rain, looking at the ashes. That was the wreck of the house; that was the wreck of the family. Looking at this wreck they came to realize how great and sacred the house had been. They cried silently; their tears mixed with the rain and fell all over their faces and down their bodies. Still in tears, he walked towards the ruins, crossed the threshold and went inside. The ashes burnt his bare feet as if in last farewell. He could feel the love of the house and he cried softly. He walked to the west wing bedroom. From under a pile of blackened wood a pair of burnt feet stuck out. This was his grandfather's grave. Grandfather built his own grave; even in death he was just as imposing. It infuriated but also consoled him.

No one doubted that it was Grandfather who set fire to the house. It was *his* house, and he had the right to dispose of his one last belonging; no one could blame him. But why did he do it? Was it in protest against the injustice of the times? Was it a punishment on his grandchildren who had disappointed him? He buried everything silently in the ashes, leaving his child and grandchildren behind just the way they had been born — empty-handed, without food or clothing, their lives at risk, and yet they had to live on.

XVIII

At the bay by the Yellow Sea the girl from Golden Corn Lane had joined the Mao Zedong Thought Propaganda Team. On the stage no one could outshine her. Her face was like a full moon, and her eyes, slanting slightly upward, were like almonds inlaid with pupils like quicksilver. Her well shaped lips were bright red. Now the times had changed she had cut her hair short, but not too short, just half an inch below her ears. It had been curled with heated tongs, and she tied a hank of hair on the top of her head into a short plait on one side. Her black hair set off her fair complexion and bright eyes to great advantage. She wore a close-fitting yellow home-made military uniform, and when she belted it up, all the curves on her body showed. From the look of her you would have taken her for an eighteen year old young woman, but she was in fact only fourteen. She was in almost every single item on the programme: announcing the performers, reciting, doing two-person and four-person dialogues, singing solos and duets, joining in the Revolutionary Dance and the Loyalty Dance. She was there from start to finish, but her heartbeat and her breathing did not even quicken; she was in perfect control. She became the biggest star in town practically overnight.

A young man in the propaganda team handed her a note expressing his endless love and everlasting faithfulness. Wrapped in the note were sea shells that looked like cats' eyes, signifying that he wanted to stare at her eternally. She took it quietly and put it in her trousers, feeling a little proud and a little amused. Although she had never had the experience herself she had seen it many times. She had peeped through the door and seen with her very eyes how the uncles knelt at her mother's feet, how mother tore up and trampled on the novel and valuable gifts they brought as if they were playthings. She had even seen the uncles cry, their manliness completely gone in front of a tender woman. What was a shabby little note in comparison! Some of the things written there were cute, yes, but compared with what the uncles felt for Mother these were paltry. Because she had seen so much, in her eyes even the boys who were a few years older than her were like children, unknowing and inexperienced. Just handing her a shabby note was enough to make him awkward and uneasy, and when his hand touched hers he actually blushed; how useless and unstylish! After reading the note several times she returned it to the young man in front of everyone, not showing her feelings at all: "You dropped this when you took out your handkerchief. I've picked it up for you." No one noticed anything unusual, and she behaved gracefully, but the young man felt as if he had been stabbed. He blushed and turned pale, and though he did not want to stay neither did he have the heart to leave. Seeing him suffering like this she felt like giggling. After this the young man tried his best to avoid her and did not even dare speak to her. And yet she behaved as if nothing had happened; she sought him out and talked to him in the most open and friendly manner. He began to grow hopeful, but he dared not be rash again. Looking at her innocent, pretty face he felt his heart aching with love for her, but there was nothing he could do. Like a plant withering in the frost, he became thin and pale, and he lost his temper easily. When she saw this she pitied him a little, and was a little touched. At night, lying in bed, she called up the image of him, thin and love-sick, and felt something stirring in her heart. She turned over and embraced her pillow as if it were her lover, and felt that in the whole wide world there was no one happier or luckier than her. She felt so happy she wanted to sigh.

The shadows cast by the moon moved across her window and entered her dreams.

XIX

At the pier the siren sounded. The boat went further and further away but he could still see his elder brother waving goodbye. His eyes were blurred; the Yangtze looked like an expanse of misty white water and the boat turned into a black dot. Brother was still waving. He wanted to wave too, but he was too shy and unused to such an exaggerated demonstration of affection. His heart was filled with love and gratitude, and he felt choked.

His brother had gone. Brother came back this time looking much thinner and at least ten years older, but his voice was still resonant. Whenever he heard that voice he felt he had something to depend on. Brother took him along to apply for subsidies from their father's work unit and from the neighbourhood committee. He rented a house, bought rice and some basic furniture, consoled their parents and told their younger brothers and sisters to behave. And then he went to the pier. He saw Brother off, walking in silence most of the way. Although he had so much to say in his heart he could not utter a word.

"What's past is past, don't think about it anymore," Brother said.

He nodded.

"As for the future, don't think too much about that either."

He nodded.

"Think about the present. Live one day at a time," said Brother. At this point the siren sounded. Brother put his hands on his shoulders, squeezed them once, and then again, and then he walked onto the gangway. He had a strong urge to rush forward and embrace his brother, but he could not move, as if he was rooted to the ground. He thought: This time Brother had not said one thing about himself. What had happened to him? Why was he so thin? Why didn't he send any news? He wanted to ask, but he did not. His beloved brother was a great person in his eyes, so much so that he dared not express any feeling of familiarity. He could only watch Brother go with an indescribable sadness in his heart. Brother's last words to him were sacred, and they echoed in his ears. And yet it was impossible not to think about the past; he could never forget the moment the house turned transparent, he could never forget the pair of burnt feet under the pile of charred wood. This scene had diminished all his previous sufferings. This scene was a burden on his shoulders; he could never be light-hearted again. The days in front of him were difficult, and he could only draw support from his visions of the future. But such visions were groundless, so even these were denied him.

The boat moved away, and the gulls followed it. The boat was now travelling on the wide expanse of the Yangtze where the waters merged with the sky, and he could not tell the sky from the earth anymore.

He felt that no one in the whole wide world was more unfortunate or had a sadder life than him.

In the vast expanse that was water and sky a pale sun was shining.

CHAPTER TWO

XX

It was a traditional single-storeyed house with a courtyard in the middle. In the courtyard there was a rehearsal room which had doors on the east and west sides and windows on the north and south sides. A large number of people walked past, not just company members in their practice clothes, but also old people and children. Water was always running from the tap; the manure cart trundled in and trundled out, leaving the ground covered in stinking liquid. The southern windows were lined with the heads of onlookers who were watching inquisitively. He could not but be scared. He turned around to face the northern windows and saw quite unexpectedly that there was a lush green wood outside. In the wood an *erhu* was playing "New Year's Eve", playing as if it were weeping. At this point his name was called and he turned round nervously and stood up. Everyone's eyes were on him. The examiners seated behind a row of desks were studying him severely. He lost his nerve. Someone asked:

"What do you play?"

"The cello," he faltered in reply.

Shortly afterwards he had a cello in his hands. He put his hand round the smooth neck of the cello and suddenly calmed down. The feeling of the cello's neck in his hand was at once strange and familiar. He did not know whether he could still approach it after such a long separation, but the bow moved across the strings and melodious notes poured forth. Even he was surprised. And then tears welled up in his eyes. He leaned his head against the neck of the cello and tuned the instrument, his eyes half closed. His left hand adjusted the tuning pegs as his right hand played on two strings at a time. The notes became more and more harmonious until they turned into melodious chords, and then the strings started to sing. He felt pangs of sorrow in his heart, and he bit his lips to hold back the tears. After tuning the cello, he sat with his hands on his knees for a while. Then he warmed up the finger joints of his left hand, and picked up the bow in his right hand and placed it across the strings. The exercise tune that climbed up and down the scale, moving two steps forward and one step back was heard again. He did not have to think; the notes flowed out naturally as if a flood gate had been opened.

All these years it had been playing in his heart, and now when the notes sounded in real life he was not surprised, just touched. The sensation of the strings rubbing against his fingers was so new that it was a pleasure. The bow was held loosely in his hand, and it moved naturally, as if it were alive. Every sensation was dear to him, too dear to be taken away from him again. The song came to an end; he stood up, placed the cello gently on the chair and walked out of the audition room. He walked out of the house, went along the outer wall and walked northward towards the lush green wood where he leaned against a toon tree and cried.

"Oh, my god," he cried in his heart. The toon tree shook, shedding a few drops of cold dew which fell onto his neck. He felt both sad and happy as feelings of joy, sorrow and bitterness welled up in his heart. The exercise tune that was forever echoing in his ears had stopped, it did not play anymore. It was as if it had at last found its way back home.

He cried for a while, then he gradually quieted down, took out a handkerchief to dry his tears, and heaved a sigh. Then he looked up at the sky, at the dense green foliage that spread beneath the azure sky, at the white clouds that were floating by quietly. He shut his eyes for a while; he felt a little dizzy from crying and wanted to find a brick to sit on under the shade of the tree. Unexpectedly he caught a glimpse of someone wearing a print shirt, and he panicked. He turned back and stumbled away.

She had been watching him from behind a bush for a long time. Seeing how heart-broken he was, she had wanted to walk over to console him, but then she thought: Since he'd come all alone to cry here he must have problems he did not want to tell anyone about, and it would not be right for her to disturb him. She wanted to walk away, but the sound of his crying broke her heart and her feet just would not move. She stood there until he gradually stopped crying, and as she made to leave, he saw her and fled. Somehow she felt that she had done him wrong.

She walked out of the wood slowly, thinking that it should be about her turn, and she walked into the house through the main gate. She stood leaning against the door of the audition room for some time before her name was called. Then she walked unhurriedly to the middle of the room and flipped her waist-long plait to her back. She stood there quietly for a moment before she said: "I'll sing 'A Painful Song of My Family' from *The Red Lantern*."[1] Her voice was rich and deep, and she spoke with a perfect Peking accent. She started to sing.

She was wearing very simple clothes — a short-sleeved shirt with small red print flowers, a pair of dark grey dacron trousers, no socks, and a pair of white sandals on her feet. But she had such graceful manners that all eyes were turned on her. Everyone was asking, "Where is she from?" They learned that she was a middle school graduate from Nanjing sent to the countryside in Ten Mile Fortress,

---

[1] One of the model plays popularized during the Cultural Revolution.

which was just west of this county town. Before she was sent down she had already played Granny Li[2] in a propaganda team.

Everyone was quite sure by now that this young woman would make it into the troupe; if there was just one vacancy, it would be for her. And if there was another vacancy, it would be for the man who played the "big turtle". The locals had rarely seen a cello before and they called it the "big turtle". No one had thought that it could play such good music; they were all stunned.

But, as is the rule, what these people figured was not exactly right. The letters of acceptance for these two were actually issued last because they had a rather complicated family background, but it was not complicated enough to make the company reverse its decision. When they finally came to report to work, the other new members had got to know each other so well that they were like family.

They met when they were buying meal coupons from the company's accounts office. She recognized him at first glance, but he did not recognize her and just bent his head shyly and let her go first. He sighed with relief when she had bought her coupons and walked away. After he had bought the coupons he returned at once to the orchestra's practice room where he was given a cello by the orchestral leader. He held onto the neck of the cello and could not let go; the bow glided across the strings so naturally that playing seemed part of his nature. The deep, melodious sound of the cello echoed around this dilapidated house and its courtyard, creating an atmosphere of sanctity and warmth.

The cello sang day and night, accompanying the sunrise and sunset in the small wood. As the days passed, people began to feel that the music, like the house, the wood, the sunrise and the sunset

---

[2] A character in the model play *The Red Lantern*.

were all natural, nothing to wonder about, nothing special.

XXI

The girl from Golden Corn Lane had a boyfriend now. He was also in the propaganda team, the one who could do a few dozen pirouettes waving a huge red flag. He went to Golden Corn Lane at all times in the day to talk to the girl, and if the girl was in no mood to pay him any attention, he talked to her mother. Her mother had grown lonely of late. The uncles who admired her so much had come less and less frequently, partly because of the unstable times in which one had better behave properly, and partly because her mother's beauty had begun to fade.

Her mother's beauty had faded, but the girl became more eye-catching by the day. She had let her hair grow long, and now it covered her shoulders. When she felt hot or bothered by it she tied it up with a white handkerchief, exposing her snow-white neck and white ears, and the small, hairy mole that grew on her cheek right next to one ear. She was sitting on a stool reading a book; actually she had not read a single line, but she pretended to be absorbed in it, and she looked so quiet, so superior, that the young man did not dare to think lustful thoughts. The young man sat there from early afternoon till dark, but few words passed between them. He did all the talking; she only answered "oh" or "no". At the end of the visit, when he got up to go, she finally raised her head and stood up. She walked before him and saw him to the door. She opened the door, turned around and smiled at him, and it was a smile so loaded with meaning that he was unable to savour it all at once. He walked out foolishly and the door was already closed; there was not a sound inside. This was enough to make him come back the next day to sit there dully, for half a day. He did it for just one smile, and he thought it was worth it.

To act with perfect decorum as befitted a real lady, that was her. To act impassioned and uncontrollable, like a wild wench in foreign films, that was her, too.

Sometimes, when there was no one at home, she had this sudden urge. She stood up abruptly; the book dropped to the ground and she was not aware of it. She stepped right on it and walked towards him, grabbed his hands and held them against her hot, burning cheeks. Then she started crying, mumbling about things which no one understood, as if she loved him desperately, and was desperately distressed. He stood there dazed, like a fool, letting her fondle his cool hands. After a long while he came to his senses; he felt that happiness was rushing straight towards him and his heart thumped. He stood up straight, trying to take her into his arms. But her passion had cooled off. She stepped back, looking at him with love and pain in her eyes. She held up one finger to her mouth and said "hu—sh", and he was transfixed as if by magic, left with but a blurred and impassioned memory of what had taken place. He could not contain the excitement in his heart, so he climbed up to the deserted Mountain of Fruit and Flowers and sang at the top of his voice. All the songs he sang were the "blue songs" from pre-Cultural Revolution days, songs like "On the Fifteenth the Moon Rises", or "Love Will Last Forever for the Two of Them", or "The Bright Sky on Double Ninth", or "Embroidering a Purse" .... People hearing him indistinctly a long way off thought it was a small animal howling.

XXII

The siren at the pier sounded again and again.

The house they had rented was old and shabby, but it was close to the river and the siren sounded much more clearly than before.

XXIII

Above the orchestra's rehearsal room was the women's dormitory. He was playing in the room, and to the person listening upstairs it was like water flowing underfoot. When she had nothing to do, she held her breath and listened, and after a while she could decipher his innermost thoughts from the music. She knew that this man had suffered unaccountable sorrows, and as the sorrow was expressed through music it gained a sense of poetry. She was twenty-four then, a middle school graduate who had done plenty of reading outside the school syllabus. His melancholy was particularly appealing to the tender feelings of a pure young woman while his almost feminine frailty aroused her maternal feelings. She may have looked weak and quiet but she had an immense inner strength and a capacity for love which were the perfect shelter for all weak souls. She could never distinguish whether the strong emotion inside her was love or maternal affection. It was a love that probably embraced all love and contained in it a sense of self-sacrifice. It was so magnanimous that it made others ashamed and inferior, and as a result gave others pain.

He was immersed in his music, completely unaware that a young woman had fallen irrevocably in love with him. At meal times, when the confused noise of footsteps sounded on the floor above and the girls trooped down to buy their meals from the canteen, one of them always stopped at his door and told him, "Take a break, it's time to eat." He did not understand that this was the first statement of love, and answered with a slight blush on his face, "Thank you. I'll be there right away." She left, but then she noticed that he did not come right away, but waited till the last minute. He only put in a laggardly appearance when the queue had dwindled away and the serving hatch was about to be closed. He bought himself a bowl of rice or two plain steamed dumplings in addition to a dish, and it was always the most expensive and least appealing dish, oone which no one else had wanted.

One day, when she stopped at the door of the rehearsal room she said, "I'll get your meal for you." And she took his bowl which was lying on his cello case. Embarrassed, he ran after her, holding his cello in his hands. But when he got to the door he was too self-conscious to go on. He did not know what to do. It would not do for him to wait for her to deliver the meal, but it would not do either for him to queue up with her together in the canteen. He sat down to play again, but his heart was not in it; he squirmed with embarrassment. He put down the bow and pulled out a pile of meal coupons from his pocket, getting them ready so that he could give her what he owed her when she came back. He waited for her nervously, and when he saw her coming round the corner towards the rehearsal room he panicked and rushed back into the room. She was there; she walked into the room calmly, put down a bowl of rice with meat and vegetables on the cello case and turned to leave. He said hurriedly, "The coupons I owe you." She stopped, turned back and smiled at him, "Three taels of rice, twenty cents." He pulled out the coupons in a hurry, dropping some on the ground before he sorted out the right amount. She took them and walked away with her own meal in her hands.

Only now did he find his behaviour ridiculous; it was such an ordinary thing and yet he was *so* disconcerted. He picked up the bowl of rice and it seemed to emit a sense of peace and warmth left by her. He felt calm. From then on he was not scared of her anymore. It seemed natural to ask her to bring him his meals and this became a habit. Sometimes when she brought him his food she stayed behind in the rehearsal room to eat with him, and they chatted briefly. She asked him how many people there were in his family; how many brothers and sisters he had. He asked her whether her parents were alive and how many brothers and sisters she had. She asked him when he graduated; he answered honestly, but omitted the time when he studied at the secondary school of the conservatory in Shanghai. He asked her when was she sent down to the countryside; she told him, and in addition also told him where she was sent and stories and gossip about the place. Her words were ordinary, but her manner was warm and friendly. She was so calm and quiet that she made him feel at ease and relaxed too. Gradually he grew to like her company. He was not a man of strong character; from childhood he had been dependent on his mother, and although he loved his brother very much, he found that his brother was too big and too strong for him, that he was scared of him, and he had never dared to be close to his brother. Though he did not know it, he was instinctively repelled by men and did not like their company. In primary and middle school, and up to now, he had never had a good friend of his own sex. And yet he was shy with women, and since he could not overcome his shyness he was always alone, though at heart he preferred women to men. He needed a strong woman, one who could help him overcome his shyness, one on whom he could depend, one who could provide not only a soft, comforting embrace but a pair of strong arms. That alone could be his resting place, that alone could set his heart at ease.

She understood all this instinctively, and loved him all the more for his weakness. Women are in fact superior to men in strength as well as wisdom, but since they do not have their battlefields, they put everything into love. She accepted his dependence willingly; it was a burden that gave her pleasure and pride. Only with this burden could her love and her life be fulfilled. His dependence also provided an outlet for her deep love and compassion, and so with all his weaknesses he turned out to have given her strong support. She wanted him; she believed that she could make him happy, and that she too would be happy. But she understood that she could not let too much feeling show, nor could she behave too passionately because that would scare him away. He was frail and shy, and he had been badly scarred. What it was that had hurt him she did not know, but she knew that the same pain would be less devastating to others than to him. He needed protection; he needed to be treated with care. The more she realized this, the more she loved him, so much so that her heart ached. But after all she was a young woman who had her self-respect, a self-respect that was stronger than most other people's. Deep in her heart she did not want him to guess her feelings, and she particularly did not want people to say in the future that it was she who took the initiative; in fact gossip to this effect had already spread from god-knows-where. Because of this she was a little angry, angry that he should be so unfeeling and so cowardly, that he should treat her like a sister. So when they gradually grew to know each other well she began to be cold towards him. For several days in a row she did not give him a call at meal times, and of course she did not bring him his meals. Whenever they met she just smiled and walked away. Even when she walked away like that she did not upset him, she just gave the impression that there was something she had to attend to. She never put anyone on the spot. When she grew cold towards him it was just as natural as when she drew close to him; it did not give rise to any awkwardness.

But when she grew cold he became somewhat at a loss, as if something was missing, so he started to look for her. When it was normally time for her to come downstairs and he did not hear her footsteps, he realized that he could tell her footsteps from the confusion of the girls all walking together. He came out of the rehearsal room, looked up and called her name aloud. She stuck out her head, smiled serenely and asked what it was. He said: Why don't you come down to eat? Not feeling well? She answered that she had asked her room-mate to bring her meal for her. He said he could have done it for her. She laughed and said that next time she'd ask him. And then she withdrew, leaving the empty window that reflected the bright sunlight. He walked slowly away, feeling that his heart was resting on more solid ground after the brief conversation, and yet also feeling a little hollow, as if he had lost something he could depend on. He went to get his own meal, which he found tasteless, and ate it sitting next to the cello. When he was half way through she came down carrying a thermos and paused to ask if he wanted some water, that there was still some left in the thermos and he could have it so that she could fill the flask up again. He said he wanted it and poured the water on the rice left in the bowl, but she was in no hurry to refill the flask, she stood at the door and talked to him casually about petty things: The sunshine was especially bright today; it was exceptionally warm this winter and so the summer wouldn't be too hot; things like that. Nothing she said was important, but everything she said fell right into his heart. When he tried to recall her words, he could not remember anything, but he felt that brightness and warmth surrounded him, physically and mentally.

She knew that she should not disappoint this man too much, that this was a man who could not handle disappointment and if she let him lose heart she would never be able to rekindle his love or to reawaken him. She only wanted to change the rules and to reverse their positions. Only then could she justify her love for him and spoil him. She did not lay out any scheme; you could say that it was all unplanned, all natural. But her feelings and her mind were so closely merged that whenever her feelings were active, her mind was in control of them, and whenever her mind was active, it was led by her feelings.

From then on she was not always the one to bring the meals, often he did it for her. And when it was his turn he always went to the canteen early, stood at the window and memorized every item of the menu written on the blackboard. As soon as he got there he took off the elastic with which he tied up the meal coupons so that he could count them out to pay for the meal easily. He looked so solemn and tense that he seemed to be carrying a great responsibility. And not only did she visit him in the rehearsal room, he often went to see her in her bedroom at night, when no one else was there. She had a gas stove which she had brought with her from Nanjing to Ten Mile Fortress and then here, and she knew how to make wine-flavoured snacks with medicinal wine. As they chatted, she made a pot of wine-flavoured egg soup and served it to him in a bowl. He felt like a greedy little boy in front of her, but he did not feel the least shy about it. Except for his mother this was the only woman before whom he did not feel shy. When he was with her he was completely disarmed; he laughed and talked as if he were a different person, or as if he had regained his true self. She emitted a sense of serenity which enveloped him, and he actually felt immensely peaceful and at ease.

During the National Day celebrations the troupe had five days off. Those who lived locally all went home; those who lived nearby went back to visit their family; the canteen was closed. But five days was too short for a few people who lived far away to go home, and they stayed behind. These included the two of them. She cooked their meals on her gas stove. They went to the market together and bought crabs and prawns which they steamed and ate with shredded ginger and sweetened vinegar. Then they bought a live chicken to make chicken broth, and fresh fish for steaming. In the five days they had ten different dishes and were as happy as if they were living at home. On the last night she suddenly asked: You cried in the wood on the day of the audition, didn't you? He blushed and admitted this, asking how she had come to know about it. She hinted with a smile. And now he remembered that he had caught a glimpse of a print shirt in the wood, so he was silent. She was silent too, and then after a long while she said that the wood was quiet and beautiful, a wonderful place. This gave him a clue, and he suggested that they go out for a walk there. She had wanted to do that all along, and was just waiting for him to ask, so she agreed with pleasure. They put on some thick clothes, left the house separately and walked along the outer wall towards the wood. The moonlight seemed to have washed everything clean: the scars on the tree bark were clearly visible, and the grass blades, with their uneven edges, were waving in the gentle breeze.

He suddenly started talking and told her every detail about himself, including his shameful experience in Shanghai, and the house on fire, and the pair of burnt feet in the charred wood.... When he spoke his heart smarted, as if pricked by a needle, but once he had spoken he felt a lightness all over his body, and his heart was as pure as a clear, calm lake. When he had finished he looked up at the sky; there was a full moon, and the moonlight was quite brilliant. He looked down on the ground, and the dew-soaked earth gave out a fragrant bitterness. And then he raised his eyes and looked into her eyes which were expressing such deep sympathy and warm love that he could not keep from shivering. He moved his lips and called her name; she answered softly. He called again, and she answered again. He saw clearly the expectation in her eyes, but he did not move forward. She saw clearly that he was afraid, but she would not give in. It was a stalemate. At last, encouraged by the look in her eyes, and because of his own weakness, he surrendered and embraced her. Only now did she stretch out her hands, put them round his neck and pull his head towards her. She held his face in her hands and stroke his hair, mumbling, "Oh, you! Oh, you!" He had never dared hope that he would be caressed like this, and yet he had been longing for it ever since he was born. He cried softly, feeling acutely his own pain and his own happiness.

XXIV

The girl from Golden Corn Lane had had numerous boyfriends and had become the talk of the town. Some rumours had it that she had driven a young man to suicide, others that she had been killed with a knife by a young man. Whatever they said, she did not kill anyone, and she herself was living a good life. She had discarded her military uniform long ago, now she was wearing a khaki shirt with a zipped front and brown bell-bottom military trousers. The higher up you looked the less "military" the trousers looked — they clung to her legs and her waist. On her feet she wore a pair of black leather shoes with a T-strap. She was beautiful and fashionable beyond description. Yes, she did have a few boyfriends, but she did not call them "boyfriends", just "friends", and since they were not boyfriends it was only reasonable for her to have a few more friends. Therefore she felt that right was on her side. Whatever people said behind her back she sought pleasure and fun as she saw fit, driving her critics out of their mind. Well, serves them right, and she was happy. She knew about the rumours around town, and she did not care a bit about them. She was broad-minded: Since none of it was true, why be angry? If she were angry it would seem that there was truth in what people said. Since someone had deliberately spread the rumours, what was the use of trying to dispel them? Would people believe her? In her clever little mind she realized that those talking behind her back were all jealous women. They were jealous of her beauty and her loveliness, of the fact that men adored her and remained faithful to her while no one cared for them. Nothing could be more unfortunate and more miserable than a woman unloved by men. And so she felt no hate for those who spread the rumours; in her heart she even pitied them somewhat, which angered them all the more and caused them to spread even more sensational rumours. Some said that she had had seven or eight abortions, and others that her mother had given her a prescription against pregnancy and no matter how many men she slept with she would always retain the looks of a virgin.

As for going to bed with men, she had her own ideas about this and no one needed to worry about her. Her "boyfriends", or according to her, "friends", all had a clear idea about it too. When they were with her, they all wanted to do it, but none of them could really do it. She was as slippery as a fish and as alert as a nymph. Whatever their sweet talk, there was no way they could cross the threshold. In her heart she knew that this was the most precious thing a woman had, it was a woman's dignity, her whole worth. She could play around and have fun if it were anything else, but this she would not let go. Her mother was good to her uncles, and they were good to her mother, but they never dared show her any disrespect. They loved her mother, they respected her, and they always kept a distance between them no matter how close they were. She had thought once that if Mother had offered them this thing the uncles would have turned cold towards her long ago and would have forgotten her as a riddle solved. A woman had to keep this from men to make herself mysterious, unfathomable, profound, to make the men stay and feel that they could not love her enough. She was wise and sensitive enough to know that her mother had only done that thing with one uncle, and that was her father. Although she had never seen him, she knew that he must have been an incredible "good uncle". Her mother had given him that thing, how could he not be good? Besides, only a useless woman would have to rely on that thing to hold onto a man, she thought. She told herself that she did not have to do anything startling to twist men about, to make them obey all her orders. There were so many ways open to a woman, and guarding that most precious thing was one way. She was not one of those useless women; even when she did not offer that she could hold the men spell-bound. That she had to reserve for someone to whom she really wanted to offer it. Where was that man? She had no idea, and she did not think about it. She was a girl who cared only for the present because the present for her was good, beautiful, full of wonder. She had not had her share of fun yet.

The game that was the most fun for her was flirting. She was not at all a bad girl; in fact at heart she was kind. She just loved playing around, and she threw herself into her games with such sincerity, such self-forgetfulness and real feelings that you could not really find fault with her. She did not intend to hurt the boys, she just wanted some fun. When they were hurt, and when she saw them suffer, she did not feel happy either, she would even cry. But the sadness and the tears were a source of joy for her; it was like someone who had his fill of sweet food craving for a bitter, sour or hot dish. What was more, it was not as if she had taken their love and care without repaying them: she gave them tenderness, and sweetness, and passionate looks, and interesting verbal exchanges. Sometimes when she met with a man not easy to deal with, she felt like a scientist faced with a difficult problem; it agitated and excited her. No matter how hard it was she had to solve this problem, and she rarely failed. It was because she understood men's nature; through her cleverness and her instincts she could see clearly even the things which the men themselves did not know about.

The girl thought that she could see through everyone. She did not realize that someone had seen through her, and that was her mother. When her mother was young she was even prettier than the girl, and in those days fashion had so much to offer. There was simply no comparison with the present when this sack of a military uniform was enough to turn heads. She understood that for a young girl to flirt with men was to experience joy and success. But when you grew older, not necessarily much older, the skin around your eyes would sag a little, the pores on your nose would be a little more visible, the creases on your lips would increase a little, and the hair at the back of your head would turn a little yellow, and flirting would become difficult and exhausting. She hoped that her daughter could first get a salaried job and then get a good, faithful husband, and then she would not have to worry.

But her daughter cared for nothing but fun.

XXV

Public opinion always walks a step ahead of facts. When everyone in the troupe thought that they were dating, they were in fact just chatting in the rehearsal room; when the rumours said that they were holding hands walking in the wood every morning and night, they had just started eating wine-flavoured eggs in her bedroom; when the troupe had given its approval to their betrothal and recognized their status as man and wife, they had finally gone to the wood for their rendezvous. And so it was that before they had made up their mind to tell others about their relationship, the others had lifted up their veil of secrecy for them, and their relationship developed speedily. After the performances for the New Year Festival, troupe members whose families were far away were given some leave, and the two of them went together back to the south. He went with her to Nanjing first and met her parents who gave them their tacit permission, and then he took her home with him.

His home was at the end of a narrow lane. It was a house shared by a dozen families, with a common courtyard in the middle. Thick moss grew on the stone slabs of the courtyard. An extremely tall and big scholar tree blocked the sunlight, and the courtyard was dark and wet all year round. His family had the two north-facing rooms. Though his mother wanted everything to be neat and clean, and was always scrubbing away, she was no match for the damp air which left dark green mouldy spots on everything. What was more, the more frequently she washed and cleaned, the more quickly the spots grew. The minute you walked into the room, a cold, damp, mouldy smell hit you. The simple furniture had faded from too much washing with soapy water and was covered in yellow and green spots; they looked like they had been skinned. Their poverty was obvious. He was almost too ashamed to look at her, regretting having brought her back. But it was necessary, for he could not make the final decision without his mother's approval. His mother's power was above everything else, and his love for his mother was above everything else. His elder brother, who was big and strong and stood on his own had to send a picture of his sister-in-law back to their mother before they got married. If they had not done so they would never have felt at peace with themselves.

His mother was seated at the square table against the wall, trying to thread a needle by a ray of sunlight shining through the back window. The sunlight fell on the cotton thread and it glowed like gossamer. He greeted her: "Mum." She turned around to look at him, and could not help showing her surprise. She was still holding the golden thread in her hand, and from the north-facing window they could hear the sound of running water and laughter which came from the area of the communal tap. Someone's head flashed by.

"Mum," she greeted her too, and her voice sounded more natural than his, more everyday.

His mother put down the needle and thread and said, "Go and wash yourselves."

He went over to get the wash basin from the rack, but she was there before him. She bent down and scooped some water from the bucket, added some hot water, and let him wash first. He buried his face in the warm water and held his breath. The water touched his face gently, like a caress. He could feel a pair of hands turning down his collar; they touched his neck first and then moved all the way along his collar to the front and touched his adam's apple. The hands were warm and firm, the fingers deft. His tears fell and mingled with the water; his heart was filled with gratitude.

At night his parents slept in the small inner room as usual. She shared his fifth sister's bed and between him and several of his brothers they had two beds and a mattress on the floor. There was no partition between the beds. He took his brothers out to walk about in the courtyard until the girls had tucked themselves in, his fifth sister then called out to them, and they came into the room, washed their faces and feet and went to bed. The back window had only a piece of gauze for a curtain, and the pure moonlight was streaming in, turning the whole room bright. He was lying on his back and he knew that she too was lying on her back. He felt unexpectedly calm, not at all disturbed or shy. His youngest brother was telling a story about some neighbour; it was so pointless that it was laughable. He laughed, and she laughed too. He felt as natural and peaceful as in the old days. After his youngest brother had finished, his sixth brother started another story, even more pointless. Before he had finished, everyone was asleep, and in their sleep they were aware of an excited voice adding colour and detail to the story. He woke up briefly in the night and turned to sleep on his side. He saw then that she was also sleeping on her side, so peaceful that there was absolutely no noise; she was sleeping as soundly as a baby. He felt at peace too and went back to sleep. When he opened his eyes again it was broad daylight. The small slice of sky at the back window was pleasantly white. His brothers and sister had got up; she was standing alone at the door, her face turned to the courtyard. She was combing her hair, which fell like a waterfall. A few rays of sunlight shone through the foliage of the scholar tree and glittered on her hair. She was combing her hair unhurriedly, stroke by stroke. Her hair wavered in the sunlight, and the sunlight slithered over her hair like quicksilver. At last she was done; she put the comb into her pocket and began to tie her hair up into a plait. Under her skilful fingers her hair was as lively as a cuttlefish jumping around. She wound her plait into a coil at the back of her head and fixed them with hairpins. Then she turned round.

The sun was shining behind her; she walked towards him with the light at her back. She had a broad forehead, a high nose and a well-formed mouth; all of a sudden she seemed to shine forth with a strange glow. He had not realized until now that she was very beautiful, a beauty which savoured of sanctity. He lay in bed dazed, watching her walking step by step towards him, smiling at him, then patting his forehead, saying, "So you're awake."

"Where's Dad?" he asked softly.

"Gone to work."

"Where's Mum?"

"Gone to the market," she answered.

He took her in his arms, pulled her towards him and laid her head against his chest. She let him embrace her, her head lying quietly on his chest listening to his heartbeat. Her fingers moved slowly along his thin shoulder blades, to and fro. He felt that it was an ant climbing in the hollow of his neck, gently tickling him. He kissed her softly on her forehead, her cheeks, her ears, and then he said, his voice shaking, "Close the door, will you?"

She got up and closed the door. The few rays of sunlight that shone through the scholar tree disappeared; the moss-covered stone slabs disappeared. From the back window they could still hear the noise of splashing water and laughter. And then the sound of the siren coming from somewhere. Both of them thought of the Yangtze that was like a huge piece of white silk.

XXVI

The girl from Golden Corn Lane spent two years at home having fun. As an only child she was not sent down to the countryside but was given a job as sales girl at a store selling fruit and sweets. She was assigned to the dried fruit counter where they sold red dates, sweet dates, *longyan*, haw jelly and that sort of sweet or sour stuff. The girl had a particular liking for *longyan*, and when she was bored standing at the counter she just picked up a handful from the basket, shelled one slowly and put it into her mouth. She pouted her lips, and out popped the shiny stone of the *longyan* which fell to the ground and kept spinning. The store bought *longyan* by the basketful, so even if she stuffed herself no one would notice. Besides, she was also covered by a category called normal wastage. Whether it was because the *longyan* was particularly nutritious, or whether it was because at eighteen the girl was in her prime, it was hard to say, but she looked fresher and more attractive by the day, like a flower bud ready to blossom. Her counter did the briskest business; it was always crowded with eager customers. A few young men who had their eyes on her were always there leaning against the counter trying to strike up a conversation. She paid them no attention, just looked into a small mirror and playfully curled her fringe, eating *longyan* all the while. She was completely spoiled by men.

In the compound where the families of high cadres in the Municipal Revolutionary Committee lived, the young men had a bet — anyone who could entice the dried fruit sales girl to say more than three sentences would be entitled to join the Sunday sparrow-shooting party for free, and that would include drinks, bread *and* as many bullets as he could use. When this was agreed upon the young men rushed out together to the dried fruit counter of the sweetshop. At that moment the girl was not looking into the mirror, and she was not eating *longyan*. She was humming a song: "Flames of the revolution are burning red; with Mao Zedong Thought heroes are bred." That was all she could remember of the lyrics, and after these two lines she just hummed the tune. This was a drum-song with numerous twists and turns in the melody, and she did not miss out a single note. The young man up front was wearing a yellow military uniform, not a "fake" but a real one, faded with constant laundering. There were several holes on the shoulders, a sign that there had been epaulettes attached to it. He approached the counter and said,

"Comrade, two catties of *longyan* please."

"Flames of the revolution are burning red ...," she hummed as she reached out for the *longyan*, weighed them on the scale and took them away for wrapping.

"I don't want that now. I'd like two catties of red dates," he said.

"With Mao Zedong Thought heroes are bred ...," she poured the *longyan* back into the container and reached out for the red dates.

"How much is it?" he asked.

"la-la-la-la..." Where she did not know the lyrics she replaced them with "la". Meanwhile she calculated the price on the abacus and then turned it around to show him: one *yuan* forty-eight cents.

He was getting upset. He pulled a five-*yuan* note from his pocket and threw it on the counter, "I need change."

"la-la-la-la..." She gave him the change. She never stopped singing throughout the exchange and never said one word to him.

He became agitated and gave the change on the counter a push, "That's not right."

"Flames of the revolution are burning red...," she had started from the top again. She came over leisurely, leaned on the counter supporting herself with one elbow and counted the bills — three one-*yuan* notes were put on one side, five ten-cent notes in the middle, and a two-cent copper coin on the other side. There was no other way to find fault with her, and he scooped the money up angrily and shoved it into his breast pocket. He could not even make her say one word to him, and for that he had paid one *yuan* and forty-eight cents! He threw the red dates away the minute he walked out of the store.

One down, another was ready to go. This was a young man in a worker's uniform, which at that time seemed to have replaced the military uniform in importance. This probably indicated that the workers had taken over the leadership position occupied by the red guards. There was nothing more fortunate than to be assigned a factory job. Besides, the worker's uniform had a top designed like a jacket; how else could you get to wear a jacket if it were not for such a uniform? He pushed open the door of the sweetshop and, looking the girl straight in the face, asked in affectedly pure Mandarin:

"Comrade, which is the way to the Mountain of Fruit and Flowers?"

She pointed her chin eastward.

"Which route by public bus?" he asked again.

She raised three fingers.

"Where's the bus stop?"

She pointed her chin to the west.

"Is the mountain any fun?" he asked casually, leaning against the counter.

She did not answer.

"We're out here on business and would like to visit some well-known scenic spot, but there seems to be nothing around except for this Mountain of Fruit and Flowers. Is it worth seeing?"

She did not answer.

"Is that the Mountain of Fruit and Flowers from *The Journey to the West*?"

She did not answer.

Finally infuriated, he flung open the door and walked out. He had not spent any money, but he had lost face, and that was even worse than losing money.

She stood behind the counter and saw all this out of the corner of her eyes. Her face was expressionless, but she was sneering at them in her heart. Who in town did not recognize these scions of high officials? But who wanted them! She liked playing around with boys; she did not care whether they were the sons of kings or the sons of beggars: it was not their dads she wanted. Besides, what is it with the kings, and what is it with the beggars? They all have to get married, don't they? Kings can have sons; so can beggars. Even kings go weak in the knees and soft in the heart at the sight of women. There was this emperor of the Tang dynasty who fell in with every wish of his Imperial Concubine Yang; he almost lost his country because of her. In front of women all men are the same. She had seen plenty of young men, they were of all sorts, and she did not fancy these sons of high officials. She thought they were too brash, like cocks which were learning to crow, the feathers on their tails not even fully grown. She liked older men, men whose age showed on their face, men who had wrinkles and a thick beard, men who had suffered and knew what pain was; those were the real men for her. To conquer such men you would need to be really good, and that would be a real challenge. In her eyes the ones who used power and social status to seduce women did not count as men. A real man would not need anything but himself — his own manliness — to capture the woman he wanted. She also despised the girls who drifted around the sons of high officials, their heads held high and behaving ever so arrogantly: had they become princesses, or queens? Women who gave themselves for money or for power should not be counted as real women either. Perhaps they would live well, eat well, dress well and enjoy a prosperous life, but she was sure that they would never know the true pleasures of a woman. A woman needed not just to be loved; she needed to love. Of course it was much more difficult to love than to be loved. She was pretty, gay, and flirtatious, and so it was natural that everyone should love her; those who did not could not be real men, that was what she thought. To be loved was thus no difficult matter, but to love someone was not easy at all.

She did not understand herself, did not know whether she was in love or not. She just liked playing around with boys, liked being together with boys, which to her was much more interesting than being with girls. It provided her with spectators for the way she dressed and targets for the special look in her eyes — it gave her a goal in life. Why is it that all through the ages it has always been one man spending his life with one woman? That is because it is the natural thing to do, it is instinct and it is meant to be. And so she felt awkward and unnatural in the company of girls, and when she was with boys she felt at ease and right at home. All of a sudden she was inspired: she thought of unexpected little tricks; her face expressed a continuous flux of emotions; her lips poured forth the most interesting talk. Even she herself did not expect any of this; it was like some kind of artistic creation. If flirting could be considered an art form, then she was a first rate artist.

And yet just being loved was boring; she longed to love someone, to love him to desperation. And so she did love to desperation, at the end of which she thought it was too exhausting, and somewhat laughable, as if she were in a play, and so she stopped loving. She felt that it was better to just love lightly. She thought: Perhaps that wasn't real love. Real love is when you become really desperate and stop caring for yourself. But she felt that hers was real love too, that there was absolutely no falsity, that she loved with her true nature. In the end she too was confused; she could not tell what was true and what was false. Anyway, she could not do without boys, she could not do without being loved, and she could not do without loving someone, so, true or false, she had to carry on. It wasn't her fault that she was good-looking! It wasn't her fault that she was lovely! It wasn't her fault that they all loved her! No matter what, she was not responsible, and so she could love to her heart's content.

But the girl's mother knew that there could only be one true love in your life, and you could only be truly loved by one person. To love only one man, and to be loved by only one man, that meant security. And yet she knew that you might not come across this one person in your whole life, or you might just see his face but never get to know him, and that would be the end of it. Or you might find and meet him, but you could never be together, you could not even see each other, and that would be the end of it. She had unbounded hope for her daughter, and endless patience with her. She had to watch out for her. She believed that if this one man were to flash before her eyes she would catch him and not let him slip away.

But her daughter cared for nothing but love.

XXVII

The siren sounded at the pier, a long call followed by a short one.

XXVIII

Nothing could be sweeter than a honeymoon. He forgot about the past, he forgot about the future, he was just filled with the concrete happiness of the present. He had never expected such tenderness. Only now did he discover that his body had been famished for thirty-three years, that he had yearned for this for thirty-three years. A woman's caresses were so exciting, so intoxicating! "I'll be good to you," he mumbled to her. "I'll be good to you," he said repeatedly. To be good to her all his life, whole-heartedly, that was the only way of repaying her tender caresses. He felt that her caresses had saved his life. They were immersed in that tenderness almost the whole night, feeling that time passed all too quickly. Their sky-blue curtains had not fully darkened when it was light again, and the colour grew paler, revealing the outlines of the window frame. Their room was only seven square metres; it was a corner of the props room which had been squeezed out for their use. A brick wall was built and a separate door made. But to them this was the most beautiful room. Because it was she who assigned a place for everything in this room, it felt just like home. And because he had inherited his mother's obsession with cleanliness, everything was clean and looked almost new, even the chipped parts on old furniture looked like decoration, adding to the charm. A four-foot double bed was placed against the south wall, so small that their heads and feet almost touched the bedends. Between the head of the bed and the wall they squeezed in a trunk which they covered with a plastic table cloth. On this they put some music scores and a small photograph of the two of them together. A large wardrobe stood against the north wall, and because of the reflection of the dressing mirror on the wardrobe the room seemed to be double its size. Between the bed and the wardrobe was a window, and under the window a square table with white tablecloth; squeezed under the table were four square stools. Right opposite the table was the door, and by the door was a coal stove, a kitchen cabinet and all the kitchen utensils. There was nowhere warmer or more perfect than this little nest. He almost thought that his pain and suffering for the last thirty-three years were all in anticipation of the reward today.

Now that he had a home, he began to feel safe and secure. He could feel the warmth and reliability of his home protecting him all the time. This protection followed him and enveloped him; it made him brave and more outgoing. He was no longer afraid of coming into contact with people, no longer afraid of meeting people. He gradually relaxed and became less defensive. His home, which confined him to a narrow space in a busy world, actually opened up his life. Because he now had a place to hide, he even began to try to make a little progress.

He started making friends. They were all from the south, and not doing very well. Being with them made him feel less inferior, and he became more friendly and at ease. He began to entertain in his little nest. He pulled the table out and placed it next to the bed, so people could sit on the bed as well. She was a good cook, and she made exclusively southern dishes such as egg and vermicelli soup, sweet and sour ribs, fried vegetables that were jade green and steamed bean curd that was white as snow. She put everything on the table, accepting everyone's praise in a composed manner. And then she glanced at him as if by chance and told him gently not to drink too much. He willingly slowed down. Her orders were extremely dear to him. He was willing to lie curled up in her bosom like a good baby and let her gently punish him. How grateful he was to her!

Her belly grew bigger mysteriously. She made a maternity dress to wear on top of her pullover, and she looked at once childish and solemn. As her belly grew bigger each day she became even gentler and tenderer. It seemed that while she was nurturing a baby she was also nurturing maternal love. He had actually learned to be naughty before her. At night, when she took off her shoes and lay in the warm bed knitting those cute little sweaters and woollen pants, he took off his shoes too, and lay his head against her protruding belly. "Don't neglect your husband because of your son," he said. She hit him on his forehead, his nose and his cheeks with the half-finished little sweaters and pants, knitting all the while. He picked up the ball of wool and pulled it out for her bit by bit, talking about irrelevant titbits which were meaningless and laughable. She did not answer him, just let him go on with his nonsense, and when it went too wild she smiled, leaned forward, bent her head and rubbed her chin against his forehead. He looked at the hazy moon behind the sky-blue curtains and thought of the long-forgotten stories he had heard as a child; he fell asleep as he recalled them. When he woke up, he found that he was lying under the warm quilt and a pair of soft, firm arms were placed around his shoulders. He felt immensely secure and happy.

The child was born; it was a girl. It seemed that he had not had enough of marital bliss to experience fatherly love. Or perhaps he had not had enough of a mother's love and was not ready to be a father. But he was by nature kind and gentle, and so he loved this little thing with a crinkled face and welcomed her into his life. As for her, she would not let him feel that someone else had taken a share of her love for him. She would not let him feel that the little thing was sharing her love with him. She wanted him to feel that from now on he would be loved by two women, that he was richer now than ever before. The love in her heart was forever increasing, it seemed to be inexhaustible. She held her daughter in her arms, and then let him hold them both in his arms, or she let him hold their daughter, and then she held them both in her arms. Because of her profound love, she who was originally mature and steady came up with numerous affectionate little tricks.

Late at night, when the man and the baby were both asleep, she watched them, and she could not describe the happiness and satisfaction in her heart. She treated them both as her children; there was a blood-tie between her and them though this tie manifested itself in different forms. The man, like the baby, was weak and helpless. She was their protector and had an undeniable responsibility towards them, a responsibility that came from the blood-tie. This made her happy. She kissed the baby, and then she kissed the man, feeling that she was the richest woman in the world. "I'll be good to you," she whispered into her husband's ears. "I'll be good to you," she whispered into the baby's ears. Be good to them to repay them for their love and dependence.

The moon in the wood had never before shone with a purer light.

XXIX

The girl from Golden Corn Lane was totally confused in love. She wanted to find someone whom she could love with all her might to see how deep her love could be.

This day she was sitting on a footstool in front of her house washing clothes. She was wearing a pair of pyjama pants with floral patterns. She had heard by chance from colleagues in the store that some Shanghai women in the newly formed song and dance troupe sat around in the courtyard wearing floral pants, that those who saw them were shocked for they looked as if they were out to entice men. She went immediately to a department store to buy some floral prints. She chose only the ones which were not glaring, and decided on one with dark green stripes and another which was pink with small purple flowers. She asked for an additional four feet of material for each as she had decided to make a sleeveless and collarless shirt to go with the pants. As soon as she got home, she cut out the material. The pants were cut in the style of western trousers, the only difference was that they had an elasticated waist. This way the pants would not hang down like a sack. As for the shirts, the waistline was taken-in slightly, the collar was cut low but the sleeves were a couple of inches longer than usual so that they would cover her rounded shoulders as well as her armpits which, if exposed, would be too vulgar. These two suits were eye-catching without being shocking. The one with the dark green stripes made her look quiet and slim; the pink one with the purple flowers made her fresh and glamorous. She alternated them, and no one could decide how to classify her. She had the advantages of both types, and she enjoyed playing both roles.

That day she was sitting on a footstool doing her laundry, wearing the green-striped suit. Suddenly someone walked into the lane, a man, tall and strong, wearing a brown military uniform but without his collar tags and hat badge. He walked firmly and slowly towards her. His build and gait were very manly, and she could not but look twice at him. Then she recognized him as a senior schoolmate who was also in the propaganda team, a drummer. She had heard that he had been sent down to the country, and later that he had joined the army. She never expected that this formerly thin and pale monkey would turn out to be so impressive. She was a little dazed. When he walked up to her wooden tub and called her name, she turned her eyes on him and, half-smiling, briefly displayed the dimples on her cheeks: "So you've come back to show off your good fortune!"

He did not reply, but instead asked her about the girl who lived next door. She was surprised. Almost every man who walked into the lane had to be looking for her, particularly one who was so impressive and who had been in the same propaganda team as her. She forgot herself and asked, "What do you want with her?" After she had spoken she regretted it, feeling that she had behaved cheaply, and therefore she was a little angry.

As it was dark he did not notice her expression. He answered in a natural tone, "Her brother and me are in the same brigade. He asked me to bring something home."

"Go on then," she said, and then regretted it again. She had said too much. After all it was none of her business; why did she have to speak!

He went into that house. A while later it had become even darker, and she had finished her laundry. She should have gone over to the tap to rinse them, but she did not want to move and just sat there. She was thinking that when he came out she would cross swords with him again, win her dignity back and see him defeated at her feet. But she would not even admit such thoughts to herself, and defended herself by saying that she was tired, that there were too many people at the tap.

Still later, the sky had turned even darker. He finally came out but he did not see her and just marched straight away. She felt pangs of jealousy in her heart and was very much displeased. At night, lying on her small pillow of bean husks, she tossed and turned, unable to sleep. In all honesty, never had a man dared treat her like that. What was he so proud about? After all, that drab uniform was nothing to boast about; if he were really good he would have been promoted to regimental or battalion commander, instead of being kicked out like this. She had noticed that he had four pockets on his uniform, so he was at most a company commander. If he had ranked any higher the news would have spread all over this tiny place, and god knows what kind of a show his family would have made of it. All of a sudden she thought of the fact that he was stationed in Shanghai, and according to what she heard the army camp was located on Nanjing Road. He had probably seen a lot of pretty and seductive women and that was why he was not impressed. This thought did not placate her, it just fuelled her anger. She turned over abruptly, thinking furiously: "And what's so grand about those Shanghai women! Do flowers bloom on their faces?" In what way was she inferior to them? It was not as though she had not seen Shanghai women, there were several of them in the song and dance troupe, all dancers, and all as thin as a stick, with flat chests and buttocks as narrow as a little boy's. Their complexion was fair, yes, but it was a dull white, unlike hers, which was fair and full of vitality. It was a gift from nature; she only washed her face with the cool well water and put on a tiny bit of honey after washing. "Face Lotion" and "Cold Cream" turned other women's faces dull and greyish-white, as if the skin was peeling, but her face was like flower petals covered in dew. Suddenly she made up her mind — she had to conquer this man. It was not because of the man as such — and it was difficult to say how much interest the man had aroused in her — it was to pit herself against the Shanghai women. It seemed that behind him stood the most beautiful, the most glamorous and the most fashionable women of Shanghai's Nanjing Road. She was filled with courage and determination to fight this solitary battle, and as a result she gained in stature in her own eyes. Once she had made up her mind, she felt herself on solid ground, and she became happy again.

She went to see the young girl next door, pretending that she wanted to borrow one of her sweaters to copy the pattern. She asked, "An ex-serviceman came to look for your family late last night, did he find you?" The young girl answered eagerly that he did, and invited her cordially to sit down. This girl, like all the other women, hated her fiercely behind her back and had called her "tart" a thousand times, but in front of her they were all a little scared.

The fact that she had sought her out was enough to make her happy and rather proud. You never know how women really feel. The young girl told her at once that the man and her brother had served at the same place, and now he had been demobilized and was working in the Industry Bureau.... She cut her short and said, "That pale green sweater you were wearing the other day, could you let me have a look and copy the pattern?" The girl was greatly flattered: Such a pretty, fashionable woman actually had her eye on her sweater! She took it out as quickly as she could, and from that day onwards the sweater became the most precious item in her wardrobe.

She made notes of the pattern and some of the stitches and then took her leave. Now she knew the basics. The man worked in the Industry Bureau, so she only had to change her route to work to meet him. The sweetshop had the same opening hours as government institutions, and she knew roughly the location of that man's house. She secretly planned the route she had to take. After that she felt fine, and talked and laughed as the occasion warranted.

Two days later, she met him on her way to work, but she pretended not to see him and walked on. On that day she was wearing a white shirt and a blue skirt; she knew that simple clothes set off her good looks to the best advantage. But he did not see her; he did not even pause, just sped by on his bicycle. She was of course a little put out, but her determination remained unshaken and she was actually in better spirits than ever. She thought: It is only right that old school friends should talk when they bump into each other on the streets; if they didn't it would be unnatural, it would mean that there was something between them which made them put on an act. She knew that if a man and a woman were too considerate to one another, there must be something between them. Similarly, if they treated each other badly, like enemies, there was definitely also something between them. If it were normal friendship they would be neither too close nor too distant, neither too warm nor too cold to each other. She had her plans made: tomorrow when they met on the streets she would say hello. This should make him realize that in her eyes he was nothing unusual, just an old schoolmate. It would also show him up as ungracious, nervous, ill at ease and lacking in savoir faire. And so that's the man who had been in Shanghai and had seen Shanghai women! She laughed to herself.

But come the next day, before she could open her mouth to speak he turned his bicycle towards her. He did not bother to get off, just rested one foot on the ground and said, "Hey, it's you. What a coincidence." He looked so dashing that she was dazed for a minute and could not but be impressed: He really had been around. His smile was warm and friendly, but there was not a hint of anything else. She was a little disappointed. And since he had taken the upper hand she was also a little angry. And having been caught unawares, she did not know how to respond. She could only smile in a similarly friendly manner and said, "Well really, what a coincidence."

"Where do you work?" he asked.

"The sweetshop," she replied.

"I'm with the Industry Bureau; Organization Department. Drop in to see me when you're free." He pointed in front with his chin.

Just as she felt that he had betrayed himself, he added, "Old schoolmates from the propaganda team should get together some time." That said, he pushed off and rode away.

There was nothing she could do but continue on her way. She looked at the pink floral dress she was wearing and felt snubbed. She almost wanted to cry.

He sped off, and after a certain distance he slowed down, wondering how he had scored in this first offensive. Her face did not betray anything, and she looked at ease and kept just the right distance, she had certainly improved from her younger days, and of course she was much prettier too. He did not know how she felt, but he had made up his mind to conquer her. His interest in her was not new; long ago, when he was still in the propaganda team, he had fallen for her. But at that time he did not realize that it was love, he thought it was hate. He hated her for her pride, her flirtatiousness, for the way that the boys surrounded her and the way she teased them like they were monkeys. Everyone wanted to be close to her, but he stayed away. Everyone wanted to date her, but he did not even talk to her. Those who did not succeed in dating her or staying close to her called her all sorts of names — bitch, tart — but he never followed suit. Later when he had been sent down to the country, he had seen her several times on the road when he was on home leave. He noticed that she had grown more and more beautiful, and began to feel that he wanted her. He often went to places that were on her way and waited for her to pass by. And yet he never spoke to her. He knew that if he did he would have been rejected and insulted. And even if in the beginning he had a friendly reception he would still have got the boot later on. She was just too proud, spoiled rotten by those spineless men. And still later, after he had joined the army and was of a marriageable age, and particularly when he realized that he could not stay on in the army and had to be demobilized, she appeared in front of him every night, winking at him with eyes that seemed to talk, flashing her dimples at him as if smiling, frowning at him as if she wanted to scold him, pouting her lips as if she was about to throw a tantrum. Having her image in his mind, no other woman appealed to him; they all looked affected, false, unwomanly. He had promised himself that he would marry no one but her. But he understood that this woman was unlike any other. She had seen too many men and been loved too much. If he were to catch her attention he had to behave differently from the others. Besides, he had to break her pride and tame her flirtatious ways. He did not know whether the rumours about her were true or not; if they were false, all the better; even if they were true, he had stayed in Shanghai for a few years and had read a few western novels in translation so he was prepared to make certain sacrifices for love. But she had to belong to him alone. Her beauty and her coquetry could only be meant for him and be enjoyed by him. Oh she was just too beautiful, too alluring. To win the future he wanted he had to make the mental preparation for a difficult, long-drawn-out and exciting battle.

They had each met their match.

XXX

When his second daughter was born he finally knew what fatherly love was.

He was like a physically and mentally weak child who needed the nurturing of a double share or more of maternal love in order to grow up. Like a baby sucking at his mother's breasts, he sucked at her love for him, a love coloured by her maternal feelings. Gradually he became stronger, his feelings of manliness deepened, and with this he developed a father's love for the baby girl. When his younger daughter spoke indistinctly and called him "Father", he was beside himself with joy. When she hit his face with her little hands, he felt such bliss that he almost cried. As for his elder daughter, though she was only two years older than the baby, he had not had a chance to nurture his paternal feelings for her when she was young, and so she was almost like a friend, a very dear little friend. This little friend was like her mother's assistant, like a smaller version of her mother. She and her mother, in their different ways, surrounded him with the tenderest motherly love. To be fair, she too had played her part in arousing his paternal feelings. Girls are born with maternal instincts, though these instincts are expressed in a childish and unconscious way. When her father held her sister close, she looked on from the side and, without any feelings of jealousy, laughed good-naturedly and happily, watching the antics of her father and sister with a mother's fondness. The look in her eyes moved him, but it was a different kind of feeling altogether. As fatherly love grew in him, so did a sense of responsibility.

He liked girls, and he had never felt sorry that he did not have a boy. On the contrary, deep at heart he was glad that the second child was not a boy. Now, there were three women at home to love him; gradually he was becoming spoiled by women.

But with the coming of the children life became more and more difficult. Their seven-square-metre room could not take an extra bed, so all four of them slept on a bed four feet wide. If they did not take care when they turned over in bed they would end up lying on one of the children. They had heard so many stories of how children were crushed to death in bed by adults that they almost never dared to turn over. And because he had gradually grown stronger, his desire for her had grown too. Though the children did not notice anything, their peaceful breathing and their sweet faces made him feel that doing something like that was cheap and blasphemous, and so he kept his urge under control. But he did not have any peace all night, and when he got up in the morning he felt slightly irritable.

It was hard to keep a family of four on the salaries they drew, and they were as hard-pressed as could be. If she had not been so good at managing the household they would probably not have had enough to eat. How to balance their budget, and how to leave a little aside for the rainy day was always a part of their daily conversation: he felt disheartened and helpless. But the worst was when they had to go on tour. Every tour lasted for three to five months, and there was no alternative but for them to take the children with them. It was an unsettled life; sometimes they changed venues every day. If the theatre had good facilities they would be allocated a room to themselves, but mostly the men and the women had separate dormitories. Then she had to take care of both children on her own, and he could not be of any help. Sometimes the children cried non-stop in the night and woke up everyone in the women's dormitory. Those who were married and had children were more understanding, but the unmarried girls did not realize how such things were, and they complained endlessly. He could only loiter outside the women's dormitory, listening to the children wailing and the women's outspoken complaints, feeling so agitated and helpless that it seemed his heart was torn apart.

The model plays[3] had now outgrown their popularity and because the troupe had started out as a Henan opera troupe it reverted to its old repertory. She was originally from Nanjing, and though she could manage the dialogue in Peking opera, her mastery of Henan dialect was just not good enough, and so she lost her status as a principal and could only play walk-on roles. The cello was never part of Henan opera, and the troupe did not have a regular orchestra. When they played for the Henan operas there was no orchestral score; everyone just did as he pleased. The cello was treated as a *daruan*;[4] he was not even given a music score and was told to play it as it suited him — play the melody, or play the first note of every bar, or not play at all. Whatever he did the performances carried on unhindered. But at this time they could not think about their career or future prospects. They just kept their eyes on the present. If they could live peacefully day by day, and if no one in the family fell ill, it was already a victory for them.

Because of this, in spite of life's difficulties and their many disappointments, they were spiritually fulfilled and they shared the same goal. Getting by each day was their goal. Since they had to face

---

[3] In the late 1960s, at the height of the Cultural Revolution, Mao's wife Jiang Qing dictated that all old theatrical works be abandoned to make way for eight "model plays". Of these there were five Peking operas: *Taking the Bandit's Stronghold, On the Docks, The Red Lantern, Shajiabang* and *Raid on the White-tiger Regiment*. The remaining works included two ballets — *The Red Detachment of Women* and *The White-haired Girl*— and *Shajiabang*, a symphonic work. Later, other model plays were also released.

[4] A Chinese string instrument.

up to their difficult and straitened circumstances, and to deal with the problems of daily life, their love was given a solid content and they had practical things to do. As a result they felt even closer to each other. The four of them lived in a tight embrace, forgetting everything else, watching the days pass slowly. When one of the children had grown a new tooth or had learned a new song, or when they had bought a live fish and cooked it well, or when they were allocated a single room with an additional bed, they felt happy and satisfied, as if it was a great blessing.

For him this was particularly true. He had always fought against invisible barriers on his own, struggling alone in a nameless despondency. Now that life's problems had become concrete and tangible, he was no longer worried or tortured. Moreover, he was not fighting alone anymore; he had someone he could depend on, a companion. And so although life was hard, it was simple, and he felt calm and reassured.

The children were growing up every day; they were pretty and well-behaved. The two little sisters could sit on the bed and play with the toy bear for a whole day. Sometimes his mother would take them home for a while, and sometimes her mother would do the same. At such times they could be more relaxed and could enjoy their intimacy, and financially it was also a relief, so naturally they began to think about themselves. Neither of them had wanted to just get by, they were educated and had their aspirations. Playing a minor role in a small theatrical troupe was definitely not a long-term solution. At this point he was told by a friend that 300 *li* east of here, in the city by the Yellow Sea Bay, a new song and dance company had been set up. It was looking for new members and was particularly in need of cellists; why didn't he have a go?

At first he had thought that there would be no way out for him, and so he wallowed in his troubles. Now that there was hope, he became scared and hesitant. He was too lazy and too unambitious a man to want to compete with others. If he were not at the end of his tether he would not try to break out. As soon as he thought of the hard work he had to undertake if he wanted to go there, and that the hard work could actually all be in vain, he was afraid. In order to avoid going he even stopped complaining and dared not be sad. He pretended to be happy to show that he was satisfied with what he had.

None of this escaped her. She knew this man too well, and at heart she laughed at him and pitied him. She did not expose his game for she knew that in spite of his weakness, he was extremely sensitive and had very strong self-pride. He had to be treated with care. At night, she stroked his soft hair with extreme tenderness; in the day she made him the best dishes and took perfect care of him. She made him feel completely at ease mentally and physically. And then she said, "Let's go there." She said it in such a natural and ordinary manner that it was as if she was inviting him to go to the market, so as not to upset him. And then she went on, "Take it as a sight-seeing trip; we've never been there before." In spite of her casual tone he felt oppressed and did not speak. She said again, "Your cello; you're wasting your talent here."

She really felt that he deserved better. She could accept her lot; after all she had never studied drama or music. She sang out of interest and never dreamt that she would make a living out of it and get herself out of the village too. What was more, she never dreamt that she would meet him and be married to such a good husband. She knew that he played the cello exceptionally well, that he was talented, and she knew that he loved the cello. Anyone who had heard him play and seen his expression when he was playing would understand this. She wished from the bottom of her heart that he could develop his talent, that although he might not have a brilliant future it would not be too dim either. However, it was not just for this that she encouraged him, she was also thinking of her daughters' education. Though the other place might be small, it was a city nonetheless, and it was also close to the sea. In the long term the prospects there should be good.

She was also thinking of herself a little. She had grown up in the city and was not used to the life style and customs of a small county town. In her heart she was always longing for city life. Besides, she was born with the spirit to constantly improve her lot; although she was not the aggressive sort she thought that there was no harm in trying hard, that even if you did not succeed there would be nothing to lose either. You should at least give it a try. And so she had to encourage him. Of course she could not tell him all this in a short time, it would have been too great a responsibility for him, he would be scared stiff by this responsibility even before it had a chance to crush him. She had better not scare him away. And so she only gave him a slight responsibility, just a little pressure, not too much of a burden. And so she just said, "I know you like playing the cello."

This touched him. He had been on loan to a song and dance company in northern Xuzhou to play in the musical *Heroes of the Prairie*. The orchestra was not very good, but it *was* an orchestra. When the music from his cello joined in with the others, complementing each other, he was truly excited. And then there was the cello solo: the strings in the whole orchestra hummed for him, the piano echoed his music with a series of arpeggios; he could hear his music coming out of the loudspeakers and filling the whole theatre, the silent theatre, and he felt proud....

He immersed himself in this memory, and she walked out of the room quietly so as not to disturb him. She had left him alone, but he could not be calm anymore. When he got really agitated she held him in her arms and encouraged him with the kindest words; she calmed him, gave him strength and made him at ease again. She said that it was no big deal, he could just try it out and if it didn't work it wouldn't matter; they were happy the way they were, weren't they? Now that she had provided him with a broad, easy path of retreat she instilled in him, without his knowing it, a little responsibility: "The children will get a better education there." This reminded him of his responsibility as a father, and though it weighed on him, it also made him proud. She consoled and comforted him again, preparing his retreat but at the same time opening up a new front for him. Gradually she laid all his responsibilities on him without scaring him away. He made up his mind hesitantly:

"I'll go. Will you be coming?"

"Of course," she said. "We'll go and see the place together. I've heard that there is this mountain which has quite a story to it."

He was not interested; he did not have the heart for sight-seeing, but he could not back out of it now.

On a holiday they went there quietly, without telling anyone. They walked out of the house and made their way to the railway station through the wood. The rays of the morning sun were shining through the gaps in the foliage; he felt happy, and actually started humming. She took in all this and thought:

It's a good sign.

XXXI

The sirens sounded at the pier. The little granddaughter asked:

"Granny, what's that sound?"

Granny replied, "That's the boat."

"What boat?" asked the little granddaughter.

"The boat that brings Daddy home."

"Mummy says Daddy comes home by train," the granddaughter said.

"Yes, by train," Granny agreed.

Her granddaughter was playing a game of noughts and crosses on the moss-covered stone slabs. She covered the whole courtyard with the noughts and crosses she drew.

XXXII

Love was in fact a battle. And what a long and fierce battle it was!

They encountered each other every day wearing a calm and natural expression on their face, but as they rubbed shoulders and then went their separate ways their hearts were in turmoil. It had been a month now and there had been no progress. He did not know what she was up to, or whether his tactics had succeeded. She was even less sure of what he was thinking. What kind of a man was he that could behave with such ease in front of her? She hated him, but there was nothing she could do. In the twenty years of her life this was the first man she had hated and yet there was nothing she could do. This feeling of hatred and helplessness was new to her and it excited her. She gritted her teeth and swore over and over again that some day she would have him at her feet. In order to accomplish this goal she planned for a whole night and decided to change tactics. The next day, quite contrary to her usual cool self, she became warmer towards him. When she said hello, her eyes lingered on his for a while, leaving behind some sort of suggestion before she let go. That day was like a festival to him. Her eyes left him with a little suggestion every day, and as these accumulated, he found it hard to control himself. When she looked into his eyes he answered her call, but then she withdrew her glance and smiled at him frankly and politely. That day was like a festival to her too. She had won the first round, but she felt that she had lost something. Because she had taken the initiative, she had shown her hand and lost her dignity, and so after a brief moment of joy she became depressed. Thinking that she might as well go all the way she started the second round of attack. One day when she looked him in the eye he detected a trace of melancholy which moved him and delighted him more than any show of passion. Because of that trace of melancholy he actually had a few drinks when he got home. She showed him a bit of this melancholy every day, and she grew pale, which made her look more refined and quite pitiable. As if in reply to her melancholy he too became unhappy, but then she livened up: her complexion never appeared rosier, and she walked joyfully on as if she was on her way to a delightful date. With a puzzled look in his eyes he watched as she walked radiantly away. As she had expected, she enjoyed this day thoroughly. She had won the second round too. But when it occurred to her that it was she who had launched the attack, that she could be seen to have led him on, she felt depressed again. Fortunately he had revealed his feelings towards the end, and that was a sort of compensation, otherwise it would have been far too humiliating. But that only meant that it was a draw: in matters of this nature she was hard on herself. And so there came the third, the fourth, the fifth and the sixth rounds.

The matter did not seem to have made any progress, except that they both knew in their heart that they had become adversaries. Since they were adversaries their relationship could not be normal or natural. When they thought of this they both felt rather proud. But then it occurred to them that the other party had also seen through this, and they were annoyed. He thought: This woman is really playing hard to get. But he loved her the more for it, and dreamt every night that he had her in his arms and he embraced her so hard that she cried out. When he woke up he found that he was just grinding his teeth. She thought: This is a rare man. And so her feelings for him turned real. She hated him so much that she had to bite her lips, and when her lips hurt she thought it was him kissing her. She was mad that he should have kissed her, but as that was only an imagined kiss, she was also a little disappointed. She thought of his well-formed mouth and his even, white teeth, and her heartbeat quickened.

And then for some unknown reason they came across each other not just on their way to work, but also on their way home. It was early autumn; daylight was short but their working hours had not changed. When they came off work it was already dark and the streets were not lit so you could only see dark shadows moving about. And yet they always recognized each other without fail, and they always pretended that they did not see each other and just walked on. As the matter stood everything seemed clear; all they needed was a word. It could be a word from him, or from her. But he would not say it, neither would she. They were waiting for each other to say it, pressuring each other into saying it. The matter stood at a stalemate and it seemed that there was little hope of a solution unless heaven granted them a breakthrough.

One evening, on their way home, they walked straight into each other. Whether it was because they did not see clearly or whether it was intentional, no one knows, but his bicycle hit her not too gently and not too hard. As soon as they collided he came out with a curse: "Slut!" But he regretted this instantly. Why did he have to do it? He could have said, "Why, the pedestrian has thrown herself into the arms of the cyclist." It would have been a light-hearted hint at their relationship, and it would have camouflaged his real feelings. As soon as he had cursed at her she retorted: "Slut to you, you son of a bitch." And she too regretted this instantly. Why was she so agitated? It was as if she had something to hide. She should have steadied herself and said easily, "What did the cyclist want to knock down a pedestrian for?" That would have made him blush and made his heart jump.

But the flames in their heart were burning so fiercely and had been suppressed for so long that they could not afford to think, they just exploded, and they started abusing each other right in the middle of the street. Because there was no reason or cause for it, and because they could not find the right words for their feelings, they shouted nothing but foul language. Words which they had never used before came tumbling out of their mouths. It shocked everyone on the street. They were so stunned at the sight of a civilized, handsome young man and a pretty young woman spitting out foul words that for a while no one attempted to stop them; everyone had been taken aback. And as they were shouting abuse at each other, he suddenly slapped her on the cheek. She felt her cheek burning, but it gave her pleasure, and she slapped him back. Only now did the onlookers come forward to draw them apart. She struggled and shouted, "What has it to do with you sons of bitches? Go to hell!" He shoved the people off, freed his hands and grabbed her, saying, "Never seen a lovers' tiff? You think it's a free show?" Her heart trembled and for no reason her tears streamed down. The onlookers scattered, laughing and swearing, and the sky was now completely dark. They did not know how long it had been when they found themselves shivering in each other's arms. No word passed between them. The moon was finally rising now.

That night, the girl returned to her home in Golden Corn Lane and told her mother that she was getting married. For a minute her mother was shocked, and then she cried, no one knew why. The girl would not let her mother cry, she talked on and on about getting quilt covers and new clothes made. Her mother dried her tears, opened the wardrobe and told her to take a look. It was filled with silk and satin and all the expensive material you could name. Her mother had hoarded these all her life. To begin with it was for herself, and when she realized that there was no hope for her she hoarded them for her daughter. The daughter took her into her arms and cried tears of joy.

That day, at moonrise, the girl from Golden Corn Lane decided to leave Golden Corn Lane.

XXXIII

Things did not work out as easily as they had imagined, but there was not as much anguish in action as there had been in the mental preparation. After a long and persistent struggle, some progress was made regarding their transfer. The song and dance troupe decided to take him on, and she had established contacts with the film studio in that city. They had thought this over carefully; only one of them could work in the theatre, the other had to stay home and look after the children. And besides she was originally in Peking opera, and if she joined a song and dance troupe she could only be a singer, and the Peking-opera style would interfere with her singing. She decided to give up her career so that he could have a better chance. She was willing to sacrifice everything for him; any sacrifice was a great pleasure for her.

As the theatrical troupe was a collective and the song and dance troupe came under state ownership, the transfer proved to be troublesome. After a long time the order for their transfer applications was finally issued, and then the transfer orders were issued too, his came first, then hers. The troupe held a farewell party in their honour, and their friends helped them pack. This was their last night here. They lay on the floor, using a few straw mats as a mattress. He pillowed his head on a stack of old newspapers and tried to envisage their new life. Because of what they had gone through to effect the transfer, the feelings of novelty and excitement had worn off, and now they were left with only the petty things: getting a house, where to put the furniture, and school and nursery for the girls. When they had talked about all this he said, "I'd definitely not have got my transfer if it hadn't been for you." She also said, "I wouldn't have got my transfer either if it hadn't been for you." They were speaking the truth. Without each other, they would never have succeeded. After this struggle they became even more dependent on each other. They held each other close, looking at the window — the curtain had been taken down and now it was covered up temporarily with a newspaper. Moonlight illuminated the newspaper and every line on it appeared ink black. They seemed to hear the wind sighing through the trees in the little wood behind the house, and an *erhu* playing there. Only now did they find out how hard it was for them to leave this place.

Tomorrow, at sunrise, they would leave this town behind, together with the wood which held so many of their memories.

XXXIV

The honeymoon was intoxicating. Though she had played around with boys for a number of years, she had never crossed the last line of defence. And now all defences had been dismantled. She had never imagined that in the forbidden area there could be such an enchanted world. This was what love should be, this was the real taste of being a woman. All these years she had lived in vain, she had played around with boys in vain, she had been a woman in vain. With the acute pain she felt an exhilarating joy in the bottom of her heart; it was as if she had been shown the true nature of love, as if a new, expansive world had been opened before her. Now she had a battle ground for her displays and for her enjoyment. Her charm was inexhaustible, and so was the source of her happiness. She could come up with countless dear little tricks, and when these worked she was ever so proud and elated. She had thought that there was just one answer to this riddle, not knowing that this was an endless series of riddles, one leading on to another. There was much wisdom here; it was like opening up a new source of the river of life which was full of inexhaustible vitality, and it filled her body and soul.

She was thankful to this man from the bottom of her heart. It was this man who had given her such happiness by destroying her last line of defence at an opportune time. If it had been too early, she would have been physically and mentally too immature, and she would have resisted. If it had been too late, she would have been exhausted with constant worry and would not have enjoyed this pleasure to the full. He had come just at the right time, when she was twenty-two, as an answer to her awakening. Heaven had really been too good to her.

The man was surprised that there was such vitality and boldness in this woman, that she should be so good at receiving pleasure and at giving him pleasure. What was more, she was always inspired and could come up with endless little tricks that hypnotized him. In that fervent dream of love they both discarded their camouflage and showed their true feelings. He loved her to desperation; he wanted to swallow her whole and his embrace almost crushed her bones. Her cries of pain and pleasure excited him all the more. He thought in his excitement: A whole year's effort had not been wasted, he had now won his prize. But even at the height of his excitement he kept his head. He started planning his next move; he wanted to tie the woman down, and he knew how difficult that would be. And yet a woman who could be tied down easily would be no fun; she would not have excited his passion or his intelligence. What he loved in her was her wild nature. He was not a man easily satisfied; he was too energetic and too talented for that, and a woman who needed to be carefully coaxed was an ideal outlet for his energy and talent. He might have to spend the rest of his life engaged in this battle. The thought excited him, but he also kept his cool. She had been used to freedom, and she had played around with boys since she was small. Even if he were a god he could not have held her down all on his own. That was why he had to give her freedom, just enough freedom to let her have fun so that she would not be bored. He knew that if he loosened the hold too much she would run away, but if it were too tight and she felt constrained, she would also struggle to be freed. He had to get it just right so that she could be wilful occasionally but would not be able to leave him; that would be the best way. He had secretly drawn up boundaries for her, and he kept his eye on her all the time. He allowed her as many boyfriends as she used to have; it made him proud to see that his woman was loved by many men but that she belonged exclusively to him. But for the admiration of other men to be a source of pride, she must be exclusively his, so he kept careful watch over her, making sure that nothing untoward could ever happen. As for her, his broad-mindedness made her feel that he was a cut above the rest, and as a result she respected him all the more. Although she was slightly restricted she accepted the situation willingly. Besides, she could enjoy basically all the pleasures available to her before her marriage, and in addition she also enjoyed the pleasure denied unmarried girls. When she dressed up, when she flirted, when she wanted to kill with the look in her eyes, he alone was worth a dozen other spectators or adversaries. She was satisfied with him, and also at peace.

The next year she had a baby boy. She did not know whether she loved the baby or not. When he cried she pitied him, when he laughed she felt happy too, and when he sucked at her breasts she felt ticklish, and so she sprayed him with her endless supply of milk and watched how he shut his eyes and tried pitifully to duck, and she could not help kissing him. But she always felt that he was a hindrance; she had not had her share of fun yet! She had just had her fill of life as an unmarried girl and had barely started to enjoy life as a newly married woman when she was made a mother. She felt that it was too much of a rush, and so she was not averse to the idea of being separated from her son. She never missed him when her mother-in-law took him home for a week or when her own mother took him home for a couple of weeks. She looked at her breasts which were swollen with milk and she worried a little about losing her figure.

She was now like a completely ripe fruit; anyone who saw her wanted her. She stood behind her counter every day, attracting a number of fools and good-for-nothings. The man could not feel at ease with this and, claiming that her work was too hard and too exhausting, said he would have her transferred. He was fortunate in that he worked in the organization department and knew a fair number of people in town, so her transfer did not pose any problem. Soon she took off her white uniform and reported for duty as a typist at the culture palace.[5] It was an easy and respectable job, and since there was not much typing for her to do she knitted. Though she could not eat *longyan* as she used to she could wear neat and pretty clothes all day long. The man asked his army friends in Shanghai to bring him a small red bicycle; he fixed a mirror in the front and put a brand new basket there. She hung a little pink rabbit on it and as she rode, the rabbit swung back and forth. After work, she passed the market on her way home and bought a catty of dewy green celery, which she put into the basket, and rode back home in glory.

She was the glory of the town, she was also its scum. People looked at her in admiration, and then they felt ashamed of themselves, so they spat at her, and after that they felt inferior for no explicable reason.

She did not care about any of this, but came and went as pretty and happy as could be, just like the sun rising in the morning and setting in the evening.

XXXV

The age of the Gang of Four was over, and then the age of the song and dance troupe was over too. Six months after his transfer the troupe disbanded. From start to finish it had only lasted eight years, not even as long as the Gang of Four who lasted a decade. The members of the troupe were scattered around, those who had the right connections found their own jobs, and those who did not had to go wherever they were sent. He had no connections, but he

---

[5] In China every city has a culture palace which provides a venue for the performing arts and other cultural activities.

had become a well-known cellist and the culture palace took him on. And so he reported for work at the culture palace and was put in charge of cultural activities for the masses.

Seated in his office watching the sunbeams moving on the ground outside, he thought that this was rather funny: for all their trouble trying to get a transfer, it seemed that everything had been done specifically so that he could come to the culture palace.

CHAPTER THREE

XXXVI

In the culture palace there was a 120-stud bass concertina, East is Red brand, one of the best, but it was lying in a corner and no one ever touched it. He took it into his own office, and when no one else was around he took it out and played. It was an old concertina: the sound was hoarse and the bellows leaked. Throughout his playing the wind hissing in the bellows mixed with the hoarse music as if it were sighing. He pressed the keys lightly and let the bellows open and close of their own accord, hissing; he could not but feel sad. He had been separated from his cello after all; this seemed to be his fate and there was nothing he could do. One consolation was that the family had left the small county town and was now settled in a medium size city, and he had a job in a national work unit. His wife was working in the publicity department of the film studio, and after barely three months there, had been assigned a flat with two bedrooms and a sitting room. Many employees of the film studio who had worked there for a dozen years or more had not been awarded such privilege, which proved that she was not only good at her job but was well-liked by her superiors. Their elder daughter was at primary school and the younger one was attending the film studio's nursery. Though he had been separated from his beloved cello, the work at the culture palace was light and easy, and there was no need to go on tour, so he would not be separated from his wife for months on end. In all fairness he was satisfied with his lot. He had never had any extravagant hopes for the future or dreamt about anything beyond his reach; peace was all he had wanted. And he was used to telling himself that things could be worse. Though he had to go without his cello, he could often play the concertina now, and he was satisfied.

The culture palace was a new building. Facing the street was the culture palace theatre where there was a ticketing office. On the wall outside there were a huge billboard and placards announcing the programmes. Under the billboard there was a small iron door with a small sign indicating that this was the culture palace. Because the billboard was so eye-catching, this sign was hardly noticeable. But once you were inside the iron door the place turned out to be very spacious. There was a big courtyard and a two-storeyed building which housed a library, function rooms and rehearsal rooms as well as offices for the leadership. Through a doorway on the ground floor you walked past the boiler room and the kitchen to a tiny back yard where there was a row of south-facing one-storeyed houses. That was where the general office was located. The department of cultural activities for the masses in which he worked occupied one room, and there were only two people in the department. Originally the two desks faced each other, but as he was not used to sitting face to face with a stranger he used the problem of lighting as an excuse and moved his desk to the west wall. And so the other person had to move *his* desk to the east wall. Now that they were sitting with their backs to each other, each facing a wall, he felt relaxed and at ease. He turned the west wall into his own corner: there was a small book shelf with some books and magazines, a little string on which he hung a towel, a box of soap on the windowsill, and also a pot of asparagus fern. Under the glass top of his desk he placed a picture of a shepherd in the field, symbolic of the wide world outside. He looked at all this and forgot about everything behind him.

People who worked here could choose to do whatever they liked, or they could choose to do nothing. He was never one to exert himself; he would rather be bored than find something to do. And so except for teaching one or two hopeless amateur cellists there was hardly any work for him. He did not really understand what the responsibilities of the Department for Cultural Activities for the Masses were. His colleague told him: Don't think it's an easy job just because you don't have much to do now; when it's time for the gala performances by the masses you'll have your hands full. But there had never been a single gala performance yet. At the moment the factories and farms were all busy meeting production targets; it was the off season for cultural activities, and he was glad to have the free time to play his concertina. The music from the concertina sounded like someone crying, but it carried a long way, particularly on a quiet afternoon — almost everyone in the courtyard could hear it.

Her typewriter was placed in a small north-facing room on the first floor. The room had windows which looked straight onto the back yard and she could hear the music from the concertina very clearly. She was sitting on a high stool in front of the typewriter knitting a sweater. When she heard the music she turned around to take a look. Sometimes the man left the door of his office open, and then she saw a pale, thin man sitting with his face to the wall. When he was playing his posture was very strange: his head was almost pillowed on the concertina and he was completely motionless, as if he was asleep. And yet music poured forth, and although it was a bit hoarse it was very harmonious.

She turned her stool around to face the back yard, as if she were watching a play. Her hands were still knitting speedily; it was a complicated pattern but she did not get one single stitch wrong. It would only be a few days before she had a new sweater on her back. And as soon as she had put on a new sweater, an old one was taken apart and the wool washed and dried, ready to be knit into another fashionable pattern. In another week's time she had yet another brand new sweater. In this way she gave herself an endless range of new clothes and an ever-changing appearance. Since the downfall of the Gang of Four the thing that delighted her most was the wide range of dresses and fashions which had become available. Hairstyles, clothes, cosmetics, everything was new, varied and changing fast. It was so hard to catch up with the latest trends that for her it was both exciting and nerve-racking. Her zest for life had risen higher than ever before, and she mobilized every bit of her intelligence and vitality. She was particularly sensitive to all the new styles, and she was expert at creating bold variations on existing styles, so she was the most fashionable woman in town and yet no one could say that she was following one particular trend. She always stood out and she would never want to look the same as another woman. Once someone copied the pattern of one of her new sweaters and knitted an identical one for herself. She took apart her newly finished sweater furiously. And after that, the other woman looked at the one she herself had knitted and found that it had completely lost its appeal; she felt beaten. Women like clothes, but often they like the clothes other women are wearing and not the ones they themselves have. But she was exceptionally intelligent about this. Like the conductor of an orchestra who could hear the music as soon as he read an orchestral score, the minute she saw a piece of clothing material she could visualize how it would look as a dress — a dress that suited her. As far as the knowledge of womanhood was concerned, she had unlimited imagination. Had it not been for her fashionable ways, this city would have been much more backward.

She had grown her hair long, and only the ends were permed. The women in town were all wearing their long hair loose, but she parted hers right in the middle and tied it into a long plait which fell straight behind her neck. This simple and unadorned style served to emphasize her shining beauty, and all the women wearing their long hair loose suddenly looked uncouth and untidy, as if they had just come out of the public baths. Her hair plaited behind her head, she was wearing a navy blue woollen pullover, navy blue trousers and navy blue shoes. The only jewellery she had on was a red necklace around the low-cut collar. The necklace was made of cheap glass beads but on her it looked brilliant, and it put a dramatic finishing touch to her outfit. What she wore was not to be measured in terms of money; it had to be measured by one standard — was it beautiful, or was it not?

She was knitting a pale yellow sweater, listening to the music and watching the man at the other side of the courtyard dreamily playing the concertina; she found it interesting. She thought: Why not go over quietly and give him a fright? The thought delighted her. She wound the wool around the ball, put it underneath her arm and walked downstairs. She passed the boiler room and the kitchen, passed the empty back yard and walked towards his office.

When she was approaching the door she slowed down, thinking how best to scare him. But before she had made up her mind she was already there. He was totally unaware of her presence; with his head bent, his fingers dreamily stroking the keys on the concertina, he strung out a very pleasant tune. She could not find the heart to scare him now, so she just leaned on the door frame and started knitting, keeping the ball of wool under her arm.

After a while he looked up and saw her. Slightly taken aback, he asked, "Are you looking for me?"

She nodded her head seriously, "That's right."

He stood up and buttoned up the bellows.

She had just finished one row and scratched her head a couple of times with the free needle. Then she wound the wool round her little finger and said, "I've come to listen to you play."

He sat down again and unbuttoned the bellows, which swung down immediately. He pushed the bellows together and lightly lifted the keyboard with his right hand. "Just fooling around with it," he said.

"Then I'll listen to you fooling around," she said as she stepped into the room, pulled up a chair and sat down.

"In that case I dare not fool around anymore." He supported the keyboard with his right hand and, as if he was tired from carrying the concertina, pushed the strap a bit upwards.

"You're too modest," she said.

At this he smiled, "It's not modesty. I'm not a concertina player; I'm a cellist."

"I know," she said. The ball of wool fell to the ground and rolled under his desk. She had to bend down to retrieve it. She knelt on one knee, stretched her arm to reach under the desk, her head tilted to one side. Sunlight streaming in through the west window illuminated her profile, showing it up to best advantage. She finally got hold of the wool, and she blew at it and patted it to get rid of the dust. Then she sat down and started knitting again.

"So you're knitting," he said. He was trying to make conversation as he felt that otherwise it would be too awkward, but she suddenly turned fierce:

"You can play music but I'm not allowed to knit, is that it?"

"That's not what I mean," he defended himself at once. But it occurred to him that she was being really unreasonable, and yet she was putting on such self-righteous manners that he could not very well tell her off. He felt this was quite funny, but he was afraid that if he were to laugh she would be mad at him, so he just bent his head and stroked the keyboard with his fingers. The music came out intermittently. It was quiet all around; there was no one in the offices next door. Everyone had gone out.

"If you want to play then play seriously. Don't fiddle around," she said.

And so he pushed the bellows together and began to play a song seriously. He felt that she spoke as though she was giving an order, and yet she said it in such a natural manner that it was difficult not to obey.

She was knitting at great speed and staring at his hands. First she looked at his right hand, then at his left hand, and she remained silent. When the song came to a close she said, "I think of all the instruments the concertina is the most difficult to play."

"Why?" he asked.

"You see, you have to play with both your right hand and your left hand, and you have to push the bellows. You're doing three things with two hands; isn't that most difficult?" She said this as if it were the divine truth.

He laughed in spite of himself and watched her knit. She knitted very quickly, and when she finished one row she stuck the spare needle into her hair and counted the stitches: "one, two, three, four..." Though she did not look at him she knew he was watching her. She had conquered countless men before, but this fond look still made her happy. She counted the stitches slowly: "Eleven, twelve, thirteen, fourteen..." She was deliberately slow to allow his eyes to linger on her longer. It gave her pleasure.

But his eyes did not dare linger on her. Of course, her silly words delighted him. Saying silly things shows that a woman is clever. A woman who always speaks wisely is in fact a fool. He lowered his eyes, and then he looked at her again. Her hair was jet black and the parting in the middle was snowy white; a bamboo knitting needle was stuck at the back casually. When she had finished counting the stitches, he turned his eyes away and started playing again.

But she was not one to listen quietly to music. When she sat in front of the typewriter and listened to him play, she was bored and had nothing better to do. Now that there was someone in front of her, and that someone was a man, she wanted to talk.

"Where're you from?" she asked in the middle of a song, rather impolitely.

He told her where he was from.

"Are you parents still alive?" she asked.

He had to tell her.

"How many brothers and sisters do you have? Are they all working?"

He answered all her questions. Because he had so many brothers and sisters it took him quite a while to reply, but she was too impatient to listen to all this, so she cut him short and asked another question. He could barely cope with this inquisition, but he did not feel at all offended, just that it was natural. Because of her vitality, the lonely afternoon had been livened up a bit. The sunlight slowly moved across the room, and the bell sounded to announce the end of the working day. They both stood up, ready to go home. She walked out of the room ahead of him and walked briskly in front. Knowing that he was walking not far behind her and looking at her, and that he was rather taken with her, she was very happy. She pretended to be busy, that there was something she had to attend to, and without saying anything to him she walked upstairs. Her innocent pretence did not escape his eyes; her lively looks stayed in his mind and gave him a little secret pleasure.

A few days later, taking advantage of the absence of his colleague, he took out the concertina. After he had played for a while, she came in again. When the people next door heard her voice they all came over to talk to her. The office became very noisy, and he was unable to put in a single word, so he just played softly. But he was listening to how she fought off all those men with her words. She was not agitated, she was not upset, and she did not say a word that would surprise anyone. Someone said:

"So, the princess has condescended to visit us common folks today!" People referred to the offices of the leadership upstairs as the upper grade and to the offices on the ground level as the lower grade.

She answered in a leisurely manner, "Yes, I'm here. Is that forbidden?"

"What a thing to say. Would you like us to lay out a red carpet, and to present you with a bouquet?"

She laughed, "Why, yes. Do you have them?" She was knitting speedily all the while.

Someone changed the subject and asked, "How come you've plaited your hair like a country woman? Are you reverting to old-fashioned trends?"

"I like it. Any objections?" she said.

"Of course not. Why not make yourself a padded floral coat to go with it?"

"Are you going to get me the material?" she asked.

"I'd love to, but what'd people say to that!" The man had set a trap.

She seemed to be entirely unaware of it: "They'd say we comrades are helping each other out."

She was not pushy or aggressive; she did not let anyone have the upper hand over her, but she did not rebuke them either. This way people would still have the spare energy to watch her and admire her while they were fighting with her. If she had used strong words and had beaten the men completely, she would have neglected things which were more important than victory. She would have scared them off too. She did not want to scare anyone off; she did not want people to stay away from her, she wanted them to be close to her. And so although she was good at repartee she was also very friendly. The occasion made everyone happy; they all took her visit as some kind of festival.

But he was not used to it. Seeing all these people flirting so gleefully with one woman, and seeing that woman facing up to them bravely and gleefully, he felt extremely uneasy. But her manners were so innocent, and her behaviour as natural as the wind blowing over the water, he could not harden his heart and despise her. He bent his head further down and continued playing, but strangely he felt that his colleagues had done him an injustice. She had clearly come to listen to him play, but now she was making other people happy. He did not know why he should feel this way, it was ridiculous, and he tried to suppress this feeling. When he got home after work, he told his wife at dinner how silly she had been, how completely lacking in dignity, that when the men flirted with her she was actually pleased about it, and so on. His wife listened and then said quietly, "We're all different. If you don't like it you just stay out of it." He suddenly felt disheartened and ate his dinner with his head bent.

That night in bed he held his wife in his arms, and then strangely he thought: What would it be like to hold *her* in his arms? At this he broke out in a cold sweat, and embracing his wife became unnatural. To overcome this feeling of unnaturalness he held her even closer, and his wife repaid him with even greater tenderness. He gradually calmed down and fell asleep.

After this she seemed to have got used to coming to his office, and she came frequently, bringing her knitting of varied colours and ever-new patterns. She listened to him play, but after a short while she cut in and talked to him. Her voice was like a horn, it called on all the men in the different offices to assemble for a verbal joust with her. Now he could play at leisure, and the hissing of the leaky concertina mingled with her unhurried replies. She was happy to be under seige, but her happiness was not perfect because he had not joined in. She could not stand having even one man outside her control, and so she picked on him deliberately:

"So, our musician does not care to speak with the masses!"

"I'm one of the masses, too," he said. He had been dragged onto the battlefield so he had to give some sort of a reply. Or else he would be ungrateful for her attention, it seemed.

"Then why don't you talk to us?"

"I'm not as good at this as you are." He was telling the truth.

"How modest! Too much modesty means pride." She would not give up.

He could find nothing to say in return. He was embarrassed, but he also felt honoured. All the others had to seek her out and challenge her, and he was the only one whom she had made a point to challenge. But he was really inexperienced in such repartee and had no idea how he should respond, so he remained apologetically silent. The others made a loud show of their disappointment, and she was very proud of herself. But she had not had enough fun yet and went on to a second round of attack, leaving all the others out in the cold. The others felt that it was not much fun anymore, and after a while they dispersed and each returned to his own office. The two of them were left alone. When the others were all gone she stopped challenging him and changed the subject. She asked him casually about unimportant things: Where did his wife work; how many kids did they have; were they boys or girls, and so on. He gradually calmed down and did not feel embarrassed anymore. They chatted peacefully. The evening sun shone in through the windows and the atmosphere was warm and cosy. Without knowing it, both of them were slightly moved. The off-duty bell rang; they stood up to get ready to go home, and when they parted company they felt slightly embarrassed for some reason.

Two days later someone came to see him in his office and warned him in great secrecy to be careful. Not knowing what the man meant he asked: Careful about what? And yet he also seemed to know, for he blushed a little. The man told him many stories about her, all with a concrete time, place, and name. The stories all began with how she fell in love with someone and ended with how she jilted this someone. To sum up, she was like a seductive siren, hankering for men but also torturing them, and she was never truly in love with any of them; it was all a game for her. If a man fell into her trap he would never get away unharmed. Reputation aside, even his life would be in danger. The stories were full of seduction and intrigue; at once sweet and poisonous, they were enough to frighten anyone. He listened for a while and then suddenly asked: If she was like that why did they all like to joke with her; why didn't they stay away from her? His colleague was thrown out of his stride and tried to explain that they were just leading her on for fun, that they were all alert to the danger. Then he added that he had told him all this for his own good and so on, after which he walked away in a bit of a huff.

He sat at his corner looking at the picture under the glass-top on his desk, dazed. He felt confused and outraged, but he did not know why. Her face gradually appeared on the fields in the picture — the face was slightly tilted, revealing the profile of a fine nose, fine brows and full cheeks. Her lips were slightly parted, saying something silly and unreasonable, and her eyelashes fluttered casually and seductively. He felt a little unsettled and brushed his hand across the glass, wiping her image away. The picture returned to normal, showing lush green fields. But from the fields behind the glass he saw his own face — pale, thin and a trifle care-worn. He rubbed his hands against his face and a wave of discontent rose in him; he felt hard done by.

The sun moved imperceptibly. Before he realized it it was noon and the bell rang for the lunch break. He got up to go home for lunch, feeling that life was being wasted. He walked home dejectedly and in a great hurry. When he got there the children had come back from school and were playing downstairs. His wife had just got home too and was lighting the stove, so he measured the rice and cut up the vegetables, and together they cooked lunch. When it was ready they called for their daughters and had lunch together, after which he took a short nap and left for the office. He tried his best to keep his eyes open and pressed his mouth tightly closed to suppress the incessant yawns; he tried so hard that tears filled his eyes. The midday sun was like a burning fire overhead. He tried to keep his sleepiness and impatience in check and walked briskly to the culture palace. It was not until he had come through the main door and the courtyard into the cool, shady doorway that he felt relieved. A breeze blew around in the building, and the coolness filtered through his pores. He was not so sleepy now, and the fierce sunshine in the back yard made him stop walking; he would like to take a rest here first.

At this moment he heard a bicycle coming up behind him, and when he turned around he saw her parking her bike, ready to go upstairs. She was wearing a wide-brimmed straw hat, and underneath it her face was flushed from the heat. Though she had on a short-sleeved shirt, the sleeves were very narrow and came all the way down to her elbows, wrapping tightly around her firm round shoulders. He thought of his colleague's warning in the morning and could not help feeling nervous and a little embarrassed. He was ready to walk straight into the sunshine when she turned around unexpectedly and saw him. The look in her eyes seemed to be magical, for he found that he could not move anymore. He stood there dazed, smiling awkwardly. She moved languidly, untied her hat, took it off and said,

"It's just mid-May, isn't it?"

"Yes, just mid-May," he answered quickly.

"It's as hot as July," she said as she fanned herself with her hat, walked past him and went upstairs. As she passed him he could smell a strange scent in the breeze, it was not soap and it was not cold cream, it was just subtly soothing. He stood there, not daring to stare at her and not daring not to look. She saw all this out of the corner of her eye and laughed to herself. She walked slowly up the stairs, took out her key to open the door, and then sat on her high stool, fanning herself all the while. Now as she looked out of the window she saw his thin and solitary figure walking in the sunshine towards his office. The sun was fierce and his snowy white shirt reflected the light; it was blinding. He reached the door to his office and felt for his key. He took out a set of keys and tried to open the door with one of them, then he pulled it out and tried another. This time he got it; the door opened and he went inside, disappeared. A moment later he came out again to pour away the left-over tea in his cup, and he put a brick against the door to keep it open.

"A nice man," she said languidly to herself. "Naïve, but intelligent," she thought as she took a thermos cup out of her handbag. There were several half-melted ice-lollies inside. She started sucking at one and then it suddenly occurred to her: I'll let him have some. She liked the idea, she thought it would be fun, and so she laughed. She put on her hat again but did not tie the ribbon, just let the hat rest loosely on her head, almost covering her eyes. Then she picked up the thermos cup, walked downstairs, crossed the sunny backyard towards his office. She noticed that several pairs of eyes were watching her behind a row of windows, and she felt that the sun-lit backyard had turned into a stage. She walked at a leisurely pace, as if she had not noticed anything. She reached the door to his office, knocked twice and went in.

He was leaning on his desk taking a nap, and he woke with a start. He saw her standing in front of him, as if in a dream, her hat cocked and beneath it a pair of smiling eyes looking at him. She said:

"Have some ice!"

He looked at the orange-coloured thermos cup, not knowing whether to take it or not. He was filled with contradictory emotions.

Seeing him scared and at a loss, she felt both proud and happy, and she pretended all the more to be unaware of this. She opened the thermos cover, took out an ice-lolly and put it into his glass. The ice melted quickly, and she put in another one. "Enough, that's enough!" He stretched out his hand to stop her from giving him any more, and his hand touched hers. She felt her heart jump. Looking at his fingers spread over the glass she thought, "He has fine hands." She then pulled a chair over for herself, sat down and ate the last ice-lolly. She put the whole lolly in her mouth and looked at him out of the corner of her eye. He was drinking with his head bent and thinking about what his colleague had said in the morning, wondering why things seemed to be different today. She was here, but no one had come in to flirt with her, and yet there were quite a number of people in the office. Because of this he felt ill at ease and decided to treat her coldly to make her leave as soon as possible. He took some document out of his drawer and read with great concentration, with his back to her.

Seeing him so ill at ease made her even happier. She sucked on the ice-lolly and licked it with the tip of her tongue, feeling it melt drop by drop into a cold, sugary liquid which trickled down her throat. Nothing was left now but a bamboo stick which she held between her teeth, waiting for him to turn around. She knew he would definitely turn around; by now she knew this man thoroughly. As expected, he slowly turned his head around and saw that she was sitting face to the window, playing with a little bamboo stick between her teeth. He was about to turn back when she turned her glance on him and caught him. He pretended to be looking at something else; his eyes wandered across the room before they returned to concentrate on the document on his desk. She looked at his back; he was wearing a dacron shirt and she could see the white vest underneath it. A few spots of sweat had soaked through the vest and dampened the shirt, which stuck to his back. The sweat spots were expanding, and expanding; it was fun. She stood up satisfied and left without saying anything.

He knew that she was toying with him, but there was nothing he could do about it, and for this he hated her, and hated himself. He hated her for making fun of him, and he hated himself for being a coward. He dared not stay in his office alone, and so he got up and went to chat with his colleagues next door. He felt that his colleagues all eyed him with a peculiar look, as if they were testing him or making fun of him, and this made him extremely ill at ease. He was by nature a loner, and whenever he was in other people's company he felt nervous, so it would have been better for him to be alone. Yet however uneasy he felt he refused to go back to his own office.

She walked upstairs slowly and sat herself in front of the typewriter. Raising one finger after another she hit the keys intermittently. In her eyes she saw the spots of sweat on his back, how they seeped out and gradually expanded; it was like a cartoon, and she smiled. But at heart she was a little disturbed, as if her desire had been aroused, and she sat there dazed. The sweat-soaked area seemed to give out a warm scent which tickled her nose. Her heart began to thump, and she became angry. She had meant to have fun but now she was troubled, and so she felt that she had been made fun of, not realizing that in fact she was the one who started all this. She hit out at the keyboard heavily, but the loud noise of typing was not enough to still her anger. She stood up and decided to give herself the day off.

He was sitting in a colleague's office but his eyes were looking across the sun-lit back yard at the second floor of the other building. He saw a pair of hands shutting the windows, and after a while he saw someone pushing a bike walking out through the doorway. Although he did not see very clearly he was sure it was her. She had left with her bike. Now his heart was finally at ease and he returned to his office. The sun was already setting and there was a patch of shade in the back yard. His heart felt empty, as if something was missing; he was bored but he did not want to play the concertina. He sat there dully for a while, and then he decided to take the rest of the day off.

The sun sank towards the west.

When he arrived home, his elder daughter had already come back from school and was seated at the table doing her homework. It was too early to go and pick up his younger daughter from the nursery. He wanted to find something to occupy himself. He looked at the laundry in the basin and thought there was too much; he would probably not be able to finish it before dinner. He thought of going to the market, but he was too lazy to go out. He told himself that it would be difficult to explain if he should come across someone he knew. And so he lay on the bed, but at once his sleepiness vanished; he could not even close his eyes. He could hear his daughter reciting the multiplication table: "Three times three is six, three times four is twelve, three times five is fifteen, three times six is eighteen..." He followed her unconsciously, and when he realized it he stopped, feeling silly. But he was still bored; he wanted to think about something but there was nothing to think about. He had drunk the water in which the ice-lollies had melted, and he felt that the slightly sugary taste was still on his tongue; its stickiness made him thirsty. He got up to get himself a glass of water. And so he spent his time loafing, and finally it was evening. His wife had picked up their younger daughter on her way home and at last he had something to do.

"Did you learn a new song in the nursery today?" he sat his daughter in his lap and asked.

His daughter sang him the new song. He could not hear the lyrics; in fact she did not really know what it was either. She could not speak as clearly as her sister; she often bit her own tongue.

"And what dance did you learn?"

His daughter climbed down from his lap and performed some strange movements, on tip-toe, which were quite rhythmical. He felt extremely fond of her and went over to take her into his arms, but she had grown impatient with him and struggled free. She went over to her sister to play with their dolls, pretending that they were going to Granny's place. He could only go to help out in the kitchen, but his wife would not let him, saying that the kitchen was too small for two people, and that besides, unlike lunch, there was no hurry in the evening, that he should go and take a rest. He did not go, just stood leaning against the kitchen door talking to her. Though his wife told him to go, she was happy to have him there chatting to her; however hard she had to work this made her contented.

"That woman in our work unit is really screwy," he said again.

"Screwy? How?" she asked.

"She came to talk to me, and forced me to eat ice-lollies," he said.

"She's probably got her eye on you," she said jokingly.

"That's not true. She's just like that, or else people wouldn't call her screwy," he said in reply, and then he told her all the stories his colleague had told him that morning.

When she heard all this she just said, "Well, some women are like that."

Her mild response put him off slightly. But what kind of a response was he expecting anyway? He himself did not know, and so he changed the topic.

At night, for some reason he dreamt that he was sleeping by her side, and it actually seemed very natural. Her fine cheek rested against his chin, and they were lying there quietly. When he woke up, the more he thought about it the stranger it seemed; he was afraid, but he was also a bit thrilled. He closed his eyes trying to recapture that dream, but he could not sleep calmly anymore.

The next morning there was a mass study session. Everyone had to bring his own chair to the rehearsal room on the ground floor. He saw her sitting a few places in front of him; he remembered his dream and felt extremely ill at ease. She did not turn to look at him. She was knitting away with her head bent; her hair was tied into a pony-tail which was pulled round to hang in front. Her white neck was exposed, and she was wearing a white necklace to go with her dress of white lace.

Although she did not turn to look at him she could feel his eyes on her. Her neck was burning hot, and in her eyes she saw the expanding sweat spots. All of a sudden a sense of intimacy surged in her heart. She did not turn back to catch his eyes, just let him look away timidly. And then her neck felt cool, as if there was a blankness. The blankness stayed there until the end of the meeting, and she felt rather deprived. She stood up, went over to him and asked him casually, "Could you take my chair back to my room for me?" She looked at him earnestly, and he could not very well refuse, so he took her chair up to the typing room on the first floor and put it down. It was a tiny room with a window right opposite the door. A calendar of film stars hung on the wall, and in a corner of the room there was a wash basin stand on which hung a pink towel. Underneath the stand there were two thermoses with plastic covers, one red, the other green.

"Would you like some water?" she asked.

"No, thanks," he said.

"You've never been here before, have you?" she asked.

"Well, this is the upper grade," he answered jokingly.

"So you've learned some wisecracks too, haven't you?" she said.

He felt embarrassed, but also touched. At this moment the bell rang for lunch.

"Time to go," he said with a little regret.

"Let's go then," she said simply and walked out of the room together with him. Her head came up to his neck and she could see the hollow under his neck at close range. His face was right above her head, and that kind of distance was in itself suggestive of intimacy. She stood outside the door to lock up, and it took her a while. He could not make up his mind whether to wait for her and go down together, or to go down first on his own. He could have done it either way, and it would have been natural, but he simply could not make up his mind. He hesitated long enough not to go down immediately, but he could not hold out long enough and finally left on his own, so unsettled that he did not even say goodbye. As a result he seemed to be sneaking away and that was what made it unnatural. She locked up, walked down the stairs and pushed her bike out of the main entrance. After she had been riding for a short distance she saw him walking in the middle of a bustling crowd, looking weak and lonely. His shirt was too big for him, and it flapped in the wind like a flag. With such a big shirt hanging loosely on his slim body, there was a sense of sad solitude about him. The solitude had a strange charm, as if it had cut out a quiet corner from the bustling world, dividing him and the crowd and gently keeping him company on his way.

She followed him slowly on her bike and rode on for quite a long distance. Suddenly she realized she was heading the wrong way and turned back cursing herself angrily for forgetting herself. When she got home her husband asked why she was late and she said it was because of a meeting. They had lunch and then took a nap in each other's arms. Even when it was just a nap they held each other close. Gradually they were both soaked with sweat. Her hand was on her husband's back, and as she stroked him her hands were wet with sweat. It reminded her of the sweat spots on *his* back, and when she thought about it now the spots seemed sacred. One man was certainly different from another. Gradually she was lost in her thoughts and did not feel like sleeping anymore. When the alarm clock rang, her husband opened his eyes with difficulty and saw that she was staring at the ceiling wide awake. He was puzzled and asked why she had not slept. She replied that she had woken up. They got out of bed, washed their faces and went back to work.

That day when he played the concertina in his office she did not go over; she just sat in her own room. By now they were both vaguely aware that something unusual had happened between them.

They were a mature man and a mature woman fully aware of the relationship between the sexes; there was no need for everything to be spelled out. He knew that this was just a game for her but he could not help being attracted to her. To her it was indeed a game but it was threatening to turn real. She had absolutely no idea what attracted her to this man. She had spent half her life in the company of men, she had seen all sorts and had tasted true love in its many guises. If he had something lacking in the others, it could only be a sense of melancholy, otherwise he was quite ordinary. She who had always preferred excitement and hated people who looked depressed had suddenly become another person; this made her angry and helpless. She could feel the power of the sense of calmness associated with this man; it was enough to quieten her seething temperament. It was a calmness she had never experienced and so it moved her more than any passion did. She had meant to entertain herself by disturbing his peace of mind. What she had not expected was that while disturbing him she had also destroyed her own peace of mind. She was too careless; she thought that it was always the men who would surrender to their feelings, little realizing that this time her true feelings would also be aroused. She had under-estimated him and was therefore thoroughly unprepared.

Perhaps all these reasons were unimportant; perhaps the main reason was simple: at such a time and such a place she met such a man; he suited her temperament at this point in time. In fact it was she who roused her own feelings. Although her feelings were roused she was not troubled by it. Her experiences had been too rich and this was just a kind of footnote in her love life. Although it was a little different from her former experiences she was sure that it did not mean much. It would just provide entertainment and exercise for her excessive feelings and charm and would do her no harm. And so she was still sure of herself and even felt a tinge of happiness.

But he was troubled by this. To him these feelings were too unfamiliar, and anything unfamiliar scared him. And yet he could not keep his curiosity under control. Besides, rationally he kept reminding himself that he could never escape from his feelings of guilt. Although he had not yet done anything wrong he worked doubly hard at home as if he was paying off a debt of sin. He insisted on doing the housework, refusing to let up, and his insistence was so strong that it seemed that he was making a mountain out of a mole hill. The sheets were no sooner changed than he took them all out to wash again; the concrete floor was washed so often it became rough to the touch; the quilt covers seemed to be forever wet. In the middle of the night, he would suddenly hold his wife close and caress her with extraordinary passion. To his younger daughter in particular he became extremely tender; he hugged her and kissed her, making her so uncomfortable that she cried with all her might. Then he had to let her go, but his eyes betrayed a sadness. His wife was puzzled and felt uneasy. Once she asked him casually,

"That screwy girl in your office, is she still fooling around with the men?"

He was startled, and then he replied unwillingly, "Just the same. She's the friendly sort."

His wife did not question him any further and changed the subject, but he started saying good things about her. When he had said too much he too realized it, and he stopped at once, blushing a little. His wife pretended not to notice and said something casual to cover up for him. He calmed down gradually and, grateful for her broad-mindedness, he felt ashamed.

But at this time he longed to see her. Every day when he went to his office he had to look at the window on the first floor opposite. When it was shut he was restless, and when it was open he felt at ease, even happy. Seeming to understand how he felt the window was always open, as if it were pouring out its feelings or exposing something to him, sending him messages across the sun-lit or rain-drenched back yard, communicating warmly with him. Sometimes they came across each other in the doorway and although neither of them said anything, the look in their eyes expressed a lot. They were both guessing at something, but they both felt certain about it too. They looked calm, but at heart they were waging war. The boring office routine suddenly became very interesting for them; at night when they thought about going to work early next morning they became excited, and life seemed to be more fulfilling. Every day, on their way to the culture palace the sun was always shining, it kept their hearts serene. And even if it rained the rain seemed to express their love. In the afternoon, many people sneaked home early, and often in the huge compound only the windows of their two rooms remained open; all the other windows were closed as if in silence. They sat in their own rooms, separated by an empty space and at the end they felt awkward. Mostly he was the first to retreat; he shut his door to go home. Then she felt bored, and after staying furiously behind a while longer, she too locked up and left. At this time they were both afraid: they were afraid to meet, and when they met they were afraid to talk, and when they had to talk they were afraid to look each other in the eye, so they avoided each other. Originally she had no reason to be embarrassed, but despite her experience, the look of embarrassment on his face made her embarrassed too.

The situation did not escape the watchful eyes of the others. They started talking about it, and were waiting to see what would happen as if it was a farce. But nothing happened; neither of them made a move, and the people, bored, invented their own stories. Of course they never heard about the stories but they could sense the strange looks in people's eyes and knew that people were avoiding them. He who had always hated a noisy crowd and had never been bothered by solitude felt now that in the others' attitude towards him there was an unfathomable meaning; he was scared and so he began to seek out other people's company. As for her, she challenged this attitude with an affected aloofness. But whatever they did, they could feel that there was a silent public opinion against them. This public opinion attempted to draw them apart, but it actually drew them together, conveying for them feelings they dared not express. The affair seemed more and more real to them, lying between them, making it impossible for them to turn back. And so a strange thing was nurtured in their forced silence and in the solitude imposed by others.

Their embarrassment was so great that it was like an arrow ready to shoot out. They were both extremely nervous and excited. He, being inexperienced, was tortured so hard that he could not sleep. She, being experienced and knowledgeable, got much more pleasure out of it but as a result was affected much more strongly.

She could see through the truth and the falsehood better than he did, and she was scared. She sensed the danger in the game, and the danger was not threatening anyone else. Frankly if it were threatening someone else she wouldn't care; she was selfish, and she never lied to herself or to others about it. She was afraid now because the danger was threatening her. Because she understood this she was scared. She could feel that her soul and her desires had been stirred up from their deep sleep; she was unwilling to admit this, she wanted to suppress it and conquer it. If she had the chance, she would go straight up to him, say a lot of silly things, then they would embrace and bask in each other's tenderness and swear to be true to each other forever and thoroughly enjoy this abnormal love. Then perhaps their feelings, not yet ripened, would find an outlet. But the silence around them, his cowardice, her fears, all these denied them such a chance. Instead they created an atmosphere of mystery which was conducive to the ripening of their feelings. She was a wilful woman; whatever she was not supposed to do became more enticing than ever, and she had to do it. Her husband knew it only too well, and that was why he gave her all the freedom she wanted while keeping a close watch over her. When she had the freedom she would lose interest. This was why she had been able to live so uneventfully with her husband for all these years. Because of what she was, although she was a little nervous, she was even more curious. She wanted it to go on so she could find out what would happen. There was adventure here, which added an unprecedented colourfulness to the affair. She shivered with fear and with joy.

He shared her curiosity too. Though it was suppressed by his cowardice, his lack of ambition and his honesty, it was there. It seemed that it was men's destiny to eat the forbidden fruit and then be punished for it.

The obstacles, both external and internal, kept them apart, and being apart stirred up their imagination, which in turn nurtured their love. They seemed to have discovered their love overnight, it shot out of the mist like the brilliant red sun. They both shivered. He only wanted to retreat, to escape, wishing that he could hide in a hard oyster shell which would see him through this danger. No matter how he yearned for her he could suppress his feelings. It had nothing to do with courage, it was just that he was by nature cowardly and lazy. As for her, she had come to a point when she had to act.

That day he was sitting there playing the concertina out of boredom. His fingers crawled lazily on the keyboard and he did not even know what he was playing. The hoarse music reverberated in the empty back yard. All of a sudden she walked in, carrying her knitting — a bright red woollen sweater which was half-done. It was an extremely complicated pattern and there seemed to be many layers; the layers of wool blended together and the sweater had an expensive look. She did not stop knitting, just kicked the door open and walked straight in. Flustered, he brought the bellows together, buttoned them up and put the concertina down. But as he put it down he felt it was not quite right and he put the strap over his shoulder again, undid the bellows and started playing. But he did not know what to play and the bellows just opened up of their own accord, the air hissing out.

"Hey," she sat down close to him and said, "you just go on."

"All right," he answered. He started to play a song he had just recalled. After a few bars he realized that it was the song his daughter learned from nursery school and sang frequently at home: The Production Brigade Had a Flock of Ducks.

"Hey, don't play any more," she said.

The music stopped abruptly. It was quiet all around, no one

came, and no one was talking; it was exceptionally silent. It was a silence in which everyone held his breath, and they felt that there were eyes and ears hidden all around them. But they could no longer care about that. He was so tense that his breathing almost stopped; his heart was pounding. He thought that she had heard his heartbeat and was so ashamed and embarrassed that he turned pale. He dared not look at her, and yet he felt that he had to look. He raised his eyes, but he gave up halfway and lowered them again.

She continued knitting speedily, and then she held onto the tip of the needle with her left hand and pulled out some more wool with her right. After this she said, "Just a broken concertina, why keep playing it?"

Slowly he let out a breath and said with a forced smile, "I didn't use to play the concertina; I was a cellist."

"Why don't you buy yourself a cello?" she asked as she continued knitting.

"What's the point?"

"And is there a point in not buying one?" she asked, infuriated.

Now he smiled: "A cello needs an orchestra. It's only when I play with an orchestra that I find it meaningful."

"So buy an orchestra!" she said, and then both of them laughed. When they laughed they looked each other in the eye and suddenly everything seemed clear. It was as if they had established some sort of communication or understanding.

"I really have rotten luck." He felt relaxed and became more out-spoken. "I went through so much trouble to come here all because of the song and dance troupe, but then it disbanded. After all it seems that I have come all the way to work at the culture palace."

"So what? Are you regretting it?" She threw a glance at him.

The blood in his body froze. He could tell that something was going to happen; he was afraid and yet expectant.

She remained quiet, just knitted stitch after stitch. After a while she said slowly, "The culture palace is all right; it's quiet. Try working in a factory. I used to work in a sweetshop and I had to stand eight hours a day and deal with a bunch of layabouts. Now *that's* rotten luck for you."

"What do you mean, layabouts?"

She glanced at him and laughed, "They're just layabouts, that's what they are."

He could not very well ask her further and yet he was still puzzled.

Now she explained slowly, "I stood there, and all these stinking men came and pretended that they wanted to buy dried fruit, but they didn't really come for the dried fruit, understand?"

"Oh yes," he said, somewhat embarrassed, not daring to look at her.

"I'm not bad-looking, am I?" she asked all of a sudden.

He mumbled, not knowing what to say.

She laughed so hard that her whole body shook. After she stopped laughing she asked, "This sweater I'm knitting, is it pretty?"

She spread out her half-done sweater and held it up in front of her face, telling him to look. He had to turn around and look.

The sunlight was behind her, illuminating the sweater, and her features could be seen very clearly. The sweater looked thick just because the pattern was in lacy stitches, it was in fact rather flimsy. But still it acted as a barrier and he calmed down and looked at her fine features behind it. She, being on the other side of the sweater, could see him very clearly. She finally saw the look in his eyes and, assured of victory, she was overjoyed. He suddenly discovered that the eyes behind the sweater were shining mysteriously. Flustered, he looked away and mumbled,

"Very pretty."

She put down the sweater and continued knitting.

Neither of them spoke for quite a while. After a period of silence she suddenly asked, "Which do you mean is pretty, me or the sweater?"

He knew that she was faking naïvety to embarrass him, and this made him angry. And yet she was really lovely, so he replied, "You're both pretty." After he said that he blushed and his heart jumped; he almost wanted to run away.

Naturally she sensed this, and so she let him off. After talking about some irrelevant household matters she took her leave. She walked straight out, without looking at him once, and this actually made him a little sad.

After this their relationship, once frozen, seemed to have melted, and they started seeing each other again. Though their chat was all small talk, it had an unusual significance. They met frequently. She came to his office almost every day, and the colleague who shared his office always made it easier for them by leaving them alone. They felt uneasy about it, but by now they were not clear-headed enough to let it bother them. And then one day he went to her typing room. It was next to the leaders' office, and since the leaders did not work office hours, and the games room was not in use in the daytime, the building was almost empty. The two of them sat in the tiny room in an empty building and suddenly they felt that they could not find anything to say. The empty space and their proximity were both oppressive, forcing them to say something meaningful. The things they usually talked about seemed boring and affected now, and neither of them could speak in that vein anymore. After sitting on the high stool in silence for a long time, she stood up. His heart contracted and he almost fainted. She was walking towards him; she had only to take one step to reach him and he did not understand why she had taken so long. He felt giddy; the ceiling and the floor spun. She was standing right in front of him; he could not take it anymore, he really couldn't, and he stretched out his hands to her, asking for help. She had just stretched out her hands. They had to embrace, if they had not they would both have collapsed. When they embraced they felt a sudden sense of relief, as if a burden had been lifted. He held her burning body close to him, and she held his cold body close to her; they did not say a word. Outside the window the sky was blue and a few white clouds drifted slowly by. His long, slim fingers caressed her softly around the neck; it felt like icy dew rolling gently around. She had never experienced such a cool caress, and because it was so cool it roused in her a fiery passion. He felt he was wrapped in flames; he was almost suffocated. It was the suffocation of joy. Oh they were so very very happy. Oh god, they were so very very guilty.

From then on it was as if a dam had broken; they had lost control completely. Their desires rose steadily and meeting in the office in the daytime could not satisfy them any more. They began seeing each other at night, again and again. After dinner they looked for an excuse to go out, and met up in some deserted spot. And then he rode on her bike, with her sitting at the back, and they went off to somewhere even further away, usually out in the country. They forgot everything — shame, degradation. They rolled under the bushes and embraced passionately. Besides the excitement and joy of love, there was the joy of adventure, the elation of tragedy and the great happiness of rebellion.... They were almost numb. Deep into the night they realized they had to go home. Parting was what hurt most; they were filled with tenderness for each other but they had to pretend to be strangers and go their own way as if they had never met before. They had to go home.

His wife was always waiting up for him, and she never asked any questions. He was grateful for her silence, and yet he also wished that she would question him thoroughly so that he could explain himself. Now that she was keeping quiet it seemed that she understood everything and was denying him a chance to explain. He even detected a look of disgust in her eyes, which made him feel even more guilty. His wife knew nothing, but it also seemed that she knew everything. It was unusual for her husband to go out alone at night, and he always went out and came back looking sad and lost. As soon as he came in, he collapsed on the bed and lay there motionless. He slept as if he were dead, even his breathing seemed to have stopped. But when he was sleeping really soundly he became restless, tossing and turning in strange postures, completely unlike his usual self. In the past, no matter how tired he had been he would make tender love to her before he curled up to sleep like a kitten and as quiet as an unborn babe. Looking at him in his sleep, she felt a deep love in her heart. Where had that peace gone now? When he held his breath pretending to be asleep, she also kept her eyes closed. Both of them wanted the other to think that they were sleeping soundly, peacefully, that there was nothing troubling them. When he finally fell asleep and started tossing and turning she opened her eyes and looked at the darkness in front of her, her heart filled with anxiety. She was a highly intelligent woman; she could see through things like seeing through water in a clear pond. Had she been braver, had she looked further, she would have come to the conclusion that her husband was having an affair. She was wise enough to see all this. And yet she was not brave enough, she had too much self-respect, and therefore she thought of all the possibilities except this one. But because she was intelligent all the other possibilities did not convince her. She was still troubled. But because she was not brave enough, and because she loved him too much, it had not occurred to her to question him. If she had done that, given her strength and intelligence, he in his weakness would have confessed everything. But she did not question him; she just watched worriedly as he tossed and turned as if in a struggle, and she could not sleep night after night.

    He volunteered to do things for her as though he was atoning for his guilt. He fought with extreme eagerness for the most mundane housework. When she was doing the last rinse and would have finished in a few minutes, he had to take over; when she was holding some bowls in her hands, he had to take over too. She could pick up their daughter from the nursery on her way home, but he insisted on going out of his way in order to shoulder this responsibility. The concrete floor was washed three times a day. His younger daughter was not a baby anymore, she would be going to school in the autumn, and yet he held her in his lap, embraced her and kissed her endlessly, refusing to let go until she cried and shouted and swore, calling him "Stinking Daddy". His elder daughter watched quietly, neither smiling nor angry, just watched him with an inquiring look in her eyes. And so he tried to please his elder daughter, tried to make conversation with her. She needed some crayons at school and he went to the length of buying her a twenty-four-colour box of water colours. But no matter how hard he tried he could not lighten his feelings of guilt. He had fallen into the greatest misery.

Even she felt miserable. She countered her husband's doubtful look with bold resistance. He asked her: Where have you been so late at night? She replied wilfully: Went for a roll in the hay stack. Because she was telling the truth, it touched her at a sensitive spot, and she shivered. But she was angry at herself for shivering and, making a mockery of her own cowardice, she said something even bolder and more unruly. This added to her burden, and being burdened was a strange feeling for her. She had never known that there was a heavy side to life, that there were responsibilities. Because she was unused to this strange feeling, it oppressed her more than anyone else. She tried to rid herself of it without success, and this made her irritable. Though she did not love her son very much she was nevertheless quite fond of him, and yet she was now always mad at him and frequently beat him black and blue for very minor things, after which she would be filled with pity and remorse, and cry bitterly, hugging him in her arms. Her son wiped away her tears with his little hands, and she felt almost heart-broken. While she sometimes compromised where her son was concerned, she never compromised with her husband. She was always rough to him: in the daytime she never showed him mildness and at night she only showed him her back. But she was soft at heart. Her husband did not understand, and because of his extreme pride, did not want to understand. His cigarette butts covered the floor overnight. However, he was strong both physically and mentally, and he finally decided to do something about it.

It was a dark night with no moon. Two minutes after she had left the house he followed on his bicycle. Because of the shame he actually cried. If she could have seen this proud man's tears perhaps there might have been a chance of her changing her mind. But he would never let her see it, and so she was destined to go ahead. He followed her at a distance. She had on a bright red sweater and was so eye-catching in the night, like a burning flame, that his heart almost broke out of hatred for her. They met at the appointed place. She handed the bicycle over to him and let him get on, and then she jumped onto the back. His tears were suddenly dried. He stepped hard on his pedals and rushed ahead. The sound of the bicycle chain was particularly noticeable in the quiet of the countryside. Alert as ever, she looked round, jumped off the bike whispering, "Go quickly," and pushed him off. He almost fell off the bicycle. Just then her husband came up to her. She turned around proudly and looked challengingly at him. He saw that the man had disappeared so he turned round and slapped her once in the face, and then again. She stood there motionless, not even lifting her hand to defend herself. The pain washed away her shame; she almost felt happy. Her ears were humming, it was like a song. Now that he had struck her she felt that she had repaid all her debt, and she was relieved.

The next day the news spread like a whirlwind throughout the culture palace. She refused to say it was him, but of course everyone knew it was him. She put all the blame on herself: it was she who seduced him, she who had her eye on him, she who arranged for the trysts; she had done everything and they were welcome to punish her. But the responsibility always rested with the man, and besides he was older than her. He did not explain, just mumbled that they could punish him or fire him. So she stayed in the typing room but he was moved out of the office into the theatre as an odd-job man. When there were meetings he set up the microphones, when there were performances he manned the curtains, when there were film shows he collected tickets and then swept the floor afterwards.

No one told his wife, but this was a small place and when something big happened it was impossible to hide it from anyone. The film studio rented the culture palace theatre for a film show, and she brought her daughter along. When she saw from afar that he was collecting tickets she seemed to understand everything. She told her daughter that she had forgotten the tickets and they had to go home for them. When they got home they did not find the tickets and so they could not go. The daughter complained for a while and then started doing her homework. She kept her composure at first, put the kettle on and collected the laundry hanging out to dry on the balcony. When the water started boiling she felt weak all of a sudden, and she drew up a stool and sat down holding her knees, dazed. When he got home after he had gone round to the nursery to pick up their younger daughter, their elder daughter had finished her homework and was playing with her friends downstairs. The water in the kettle was boiling so hard that it did not whistle anymore; the steam pushed at the cover, which rattled. His wife sat in a daze with her back to the stove. He quickly poured the water into the thermos, but there was only enough left to fill half a bottle. He said timidly, "The water's boiled."

She shivered. Then she turned round to look at him and forced a smile. She pushed her hands against her knees and stood up, saying, "Time to cook."

"I'll do it," he said. He measured out the rice, washed it and put it on the stove. And then he started cutting the meat and the vegetables, busying himself.

She retired to the kitchen door. Leaning on the door watching him work, she felt so sad that she could no longer hold back her tears.

He dared not look up; his hands were shaking and the knife sawed backwards and forwards at the meat without cutting it. His tears gushed out and he was not quick enough to brush them aside, so they fell on the chopping board.

They cried silently for a while. She calmed down first, wiped her tears and pushed him away from the chopping board, saying, "I'll do it."

He held on for a while but was not as persistent as her, so he stepped aside. He dried his tears, but he still dared not look at her. The knife clicked against the chopping board.

They did not speak until dinner. After dinner, when the children had gone to bed, she went into their bedroom, and he followed. Waiting for her judgment, he felt tense and nervous. He almost wished that she would turn around and berate him or even hit him in the mouth. But she had decided to be silent, and the silence was more oppressive to him than any punishment; it suffocated him. She knew he was standing behind her, waiting for her to speak, but she was waiting for him. She did not mean to punish him; she just could not speak because she did not know what to say. If she admitted that she knew something it would be more than recognizing her own doubts: if she had such doubts it meant she had no confidence either in her husband or in herself. What is more pitiable than having no self-confidence?

It was a stalemate, and finally he conceded. He mumbled, "I'm a beast." She shook violently. Though in her heart she knew it, hearing him say it meant that the last trace of illusion had been wiped out even for a woman as practical as her. Now there was no escape. She made an effort to calm down and asked,

"How can you be a beast?"

He was almost begging for mercy, but she would not let him off, she was waiting for him to confess every detail. He had already confessed once to the leadership, and now it was to be a second time. Every confession was a torture. He had to tell others what they themselves learned only in silence, what they were too ashamed to speak of between themselves. Now he had to tell every detail. He was filled with shame and degradation; he felt that he had no dignity left.

She propped the bedbrush she was holding in her hand against the edge of the bed and leaned lightly on it for support, waiting. There was something threatening in her patience.

He could only tell her everything, from beginning to end.

When he was talking she did not turn to look at him. Every word he said fell clearly on her ears and into a barren heart.

He had finished and waited for her verdict.

At last she weakened. She turned sideways and sat down on the bed, exhausted.

He was also exhausted, but he had to stand.

She looked up and glanced at him from head to toe, then she asked slowly, "What are you going to do?"

He had not expected such a question and did not know what to say.

She waited, and then asked, "Is she going to marry you?"

He was taken aback. They had never thought about this. They each had their own life and had never considered this possibility and so neither of them had any such hope. He answered honestly, "We had never thought about that."

"We!" She repeated the word, smiling bitterly.

He was utterly ashamed and wished there was a hole in the ground so that he could hide.

"I — believe in you," she said. "I believe that you care for our relationship and our family." She looked around the room slowly and tears welled up in her eyes. "I believe that you did it because you lost your head. I hope you will come to your senses. There's nothing we can do about what has happened, so let it pass. But in the future — I — hope that you can promise..." She could not carry on. Her words were meant more for herself than for him. She was telling herself not to lose heart, not to feel too hurt and too hopeless. She had to give herself encouragement because in this battle she was alone.

He had never expected her to be so merciful, and he wept in gratitude. He rushed into her arms and knelt down, embracing her cold knees. Her trousers were thin, and he could feel her knees shaking. He was heart-broken. Now he realized how great her love was and how lowly and shameful all that was in comparison. He buried his face between her knees and cried loudly, saying repeatedly, "Give me a chance, give me a chance." He was helplessly ashamed of himself; he despised himself. And because of that she seemed too lofty for him, too distant. He too was alone.

She took his head into her arms and brushed her lips against his tangled hair. She loved him so much, she cared so desperately for him, but from now on her heart would never be whole again; there was a crack which could not be mended. She cried secretly for her broken heart. No one knew her pain. And no one knew his pain.

He felt guilty, he had sinned, he was ashamed, but all this was not as painful as the prospect of not seeing her again. At a time like this he wanted to see her most, and he missed her most. In this world only he and she were equals, no one but she shared his feelings, they were both sinners. His yearning for her made every other torture seem commonplace. He recalled again and again how he had embraced her; the warmth of her body went straight to his soul. He felt giddy just thinking about it. And because it was not to be he became agitated. He grew thin and melancholy. He was willing to pay any price to see her just one more time. But he did not have the courage, and he did not know what he could do, so he just brooded about it and tortured himself.

One day after the last film show in the afternoon, when the audience had left, the workers began to clean the theatre. He took a small broom to sweep the ten rows of seats in front. The broom was short and he had to bend low. In this posture he could not rid himself of his sense of shame, but he was also glad that with his head bent he would not see anyone. And so he bent low, moving forward slowly, from left to right, and at the end of the row he straightened himself and walked forward and started from right to left. After he had finished a row, he stood up and froze in his tracks. Across the dusty theatre he saw her standing silently at the last row.

This was the first time he had seen her since he fled in panic that night. She looked much thinner, and a lot quieter. She stood there giving an impression of calm and melancholy which she had never had before. He looked at her from afar, not daring to come close. The workers were all sweeping the floor, talking loudly. The dust they had brushed up filled the empty theatre, which was also reverberating with the vulgar jokes they told.

She looked at him from afar and felt that he was so thin that only his soul was left. She felt her heart breaking into small pieces. She had never known what it was like to be heart-broken; she only broke other people's hearts. She was too healthy then, too full of vitality. Pain had weakened her and made her purer than before.

Across a noisy and dirty theatre they looked at each other in silence. Their souls escaped their bodies and flew over all the obstacles to embrace tightly. They both experienced this embrace; it was more tantalizing, more moving than ever before. Pain and separation had drawn them together. What was originally a game had turned real; they were really in love.

They had suddenly experienced true love.

The next morning he was sitting in the wings playing the concertina sadly. The sorrow and disappointments he had experienced all his life surged up inside him. There was no future for him, so he could only look back. And since he was so depressed he only recalled the unpleasant things. This made him even more gloomy and dejected. He was just stretching out his life; he was not interested in living anymore.

The theatre was not lit; it was dark all around and occasionally a word or two came from the front or back stage. Suddenly, the curtain at the exit by the side of the stage was lifted. A ray of light shone through, and then it was dark again. Someone walked very fast up the stairs onto the stage and following the hoarse music came towards him and whispered in his ear, "To the fly gallery." And then she walked along the cyclorama to the other side of the stage and disappeared in the darkness.

He did not stop playing, but he was shaking all over; his knees knocked against each other and his teeth were chattering. He played for a while longer and finally could not hold out. He stopped, put the concertina down softly and walked about on the stage trying to look casual. He looked left and right, and then rushed in one stride towards the dark walkway that led to the fly gallery.

The walkway was pitch black and very narrow, and the steps were very high. He climbed up on all fours, and whenever he passed a compartment batten there was a dim light which made him break out in a cold sweat. The dim light illuminated his stealthy look and he felt so mean and low that he wanted to cry. But none of that mattered anymore. He climbed up step by step. He had never been so determined in his life; it seemed that something up there was calling for him, summoning him, something he could not and would not resist. He finally came to the highest level where he could see clearly. He was standing on one side of the narrow fly gallery, and underneath him was an empty stage; someone was talking and the sound echoed loudly across the stage. She was standing on the other side of the fly gallery and started to walk towards him. He too moved towards her. The wings were hung underneath them and they felt that they were walking in the clouds. At last they came together, their hands pitch black and their faces covered in dust. They embraced tightly, wishing that they could merge into each other's body. She cried, making a low noise. He immediately covered her mouth with his hand; he felt her biting into his palm, her sharp teeth cutting into his flesh. And then he cried, and she covered his mouth with her hands so that he would not make a noise. In this empty space the smallest sound would create a loud echo. They cried with their hands on each other's mouth. They felt that there were just the two of them left in the whole wide world, that they had to take care of each other, that they were like a small boat adrift in the open sea. Misery had changed her; she had become gentle. Desperation had changed him; for the moment he had become determined. They stood on the quivering fly gallery above the empty stage, holding their breath, suppressing their sobs, embracing each other and completely forgetting the time.

They began to see each other again. They had no morals left, and no shame. They chose to degrade themselves and did not think of themselves as respectable people anymore. This was the only course left to them; there was no other way out. And yet it was much more difficult for them to avoid being recognized now. She who had always been notorious was now known to everyone in the city, and this made him notorious too. They went further and further from the city and met at more and more deserted places; fixing a rendezvous demanded all their imagination. And then one afternoon they went to the Mountain of Fruit and Flowers where there was actually no fruit and no flowers; it was just a barren mountain.

The trees were few, the grass yellow, for it was a late autumn day. The wind sighed sadly through the trees. They sat on the grass on the western side of the mountain. The withered grass which came up to their waist was crushed on the ground and turned into a soft mattress. They held each other close, lying curled up on the grass and whispering silly, desperate words. The sun moved westward gradually to their side of the mountain and when it shone on them, it was already sunset.

They almost fell asleep. When they were woken by the cold autumn wind it was twilight, and they hurriedly climbed down the mountain. The way down was rough, and she was wearing high-heeled shoes, so he supported her. But she was too heavy for him, and he actually had to lean on her, so they supported each other as they stumbled downhill. Their clothes, soaked through with sweat, made them feel cold in the wind. The wind blew sadly, it was like an ill omen.

They finally made it to the foot of the mountain before dark. They parted without even looking at each other and went home. At home it was peaceful; nothing had happened. His wife always looked calm and this filled his heart with remorse; he could only seal up his filthy heart even more tightly. He wanted to swear never to do it again, but he dared not, for even he could not believe in himself. His self-confidence had collapsed, his will had collapsed, he was only strong where one thing was concerned — his sinful relationship with her.

Some time after his downgrading to an odd-job man, he was transferred back to the office to show that the leadership was anxious to cure him and was not prejudiced against him. Now that he was back in his office he saw her frequently on his way to and from work. Originally he had thought that not seeing each other was painful, but now he realized that it was even more painful to pretend not to see each other. Whenever he saw her red bicycle, now faded in colour, his heart contracted. He was frequently worried that his heart would just stop and put an end to all this, and then he thought pessimistically that this might not be an unfortunate conclusion. And then gradually his heart became numb; he did not shiver anymore, he did not feel the misery of not being allowed to cry or to speak. On the contrary he was glad that he could see her regularly, that they could meet secretly. It was the happiness of an unfeeling conscience, the happiness of sin. His mind had also stopped working and he just lived from day to day. But after he had been with her, when he lay at night beside his wife feeling the warmth of her body, he felt his heart had been torn asunder. He pulled at his hair, which came out in hanks. In the morning, when his wife saw the hair on his pillow, she could feel her hate as well as her love for him. She knew that the man could not save himself now, that she had to give him a hand. She wrote to both their families and said that they wanted to return to the south and asked their relatives and friends for help. And with some connections established through old schoolmates she found a work unit in Nanjing which agreed to take them on. She knew that a transfer was difficult, that it was a long and hard road and she might not even succeed. But she had to put a tangible distance between them, otherwise they would not be parted — she knew him only too well. Besides, the other woman was so determined and so strong. They had never met, but they could sense each other's presence, that they were in silent combat. They were fighting for a weak, cowardly man, a man who was in fact not worthy of their love. But when a woman loves a man, it is not for himself but for the realization of her own ideals of love. For these ideals a woman would give everything, she would sacrifice herself.

She loved him, this would never change. He was her only love. She had never loved anyone like this before; her love for him had changed her personality. Why must it be him? She did not know the reasons. Perhaps she had come to a point in her life when real love had to awaken, and the awakening demanded that she fulfil her love with a man. He was there. It was both his great fortune and his great misfortune. But whatever it was, she was truly in love with him. Even her husband saw it though he would not admit it. He would not admit that there was another man in this world who could compete with him; he would not admit that she could belong to any other man but him. He beat her, but she neither cried nor shouted, and when he really beat her hard she said she wanted a divorce. He pulled out the kitchen knife from under the chopping board and said, "All right, you divorce me, and I'll chop him in pieces." The knife shone, so did his eyes. She believed him and she was scared. It scared her all the more that *his* life, not hers, was threatened. She loved him so much she could not do without him now. From then on she dared not mention the word "divorce" to her husband, but she started asking him about it.

"Let's run away," she begged him.

"Where can we go, my darling?" His heart was bitter as gall.

"We'll go somewhere far away," she held him tight.

"My darling!" He kissed her fervently. But the kisses made her realize that they could not run away. Her heart too was bitter as gall.

Someone found out that they had been meeting in secret and he was again sent to sweep the floor in the theatre. A pile of self-criticism was put into his dossier; his heart had already been besmirched. His wife tried her best to speed up the transfer. He knew that he would have to leave this place and so they met much more often. Her husband beat her more and more frequently, and so she pressed him, "Let's get divorced."

"They won't agree to it, baby!" He did not understand how a man could find himself in such a hopeless position.

"If one party insists then they'd grant a divorce. We'd only have to insist." She tried to encourage him.

"Baby, Baby!" He caressed her fervently, and the caresses told her that divorce was also impossible.

He could not leave her, but he could not leave his wife and daughters either. His daughters had turned out to be so lovely: the elder had jumped one grade and was accepted by the best middle school in the city, and the younger was as pretty as could be. When he thought about his younger daughter his heart contracted. He was destined for misery; he had to be miserable the whole of his life. But a whole life was so long, how could he stand it! He dared not think about his life, he could only live in the present. With her in his arms he shut his eyes, shutting out everything and every thought.

In this way the days passed. They met while the transfer was being processed. Gradually the transfer became possible and the other work unit asked him to go there for an interview. In the spring festival he applied for home leave (granted once every four years) to attend the interview. He was gone for sixteen days and towards the end she could not hold out anymore. In the last three days she went to the railway station every evening to wait at the exit. There was only one train a day from the provincial capital, and she waited till everyone had come out before she left. On the afternoon of the third day he finally came out. He was holding the luggage in one hand and his daughter's hand in the other. His daughter walked hand in hand with her elder sister who was holding the hand of his wife. He turned pale; his hand shook, and the shaking was transmitted through his daughters to the hand of his wife. His wife turned pale too. She knew that she was there, that she must be nearby, but she looked straight ahead and walked on as if nothing had happened. She was standing behind the barriers at the exit, looking straight at him, trying to catch his eye. He tried to avoid her, but finally he could no longer avoid her and he looked at her pleadingly. She watched him go, her heart filled with both love and hate, and tears streamed down her face.

The day finally came when the transfer order was issued. It was for him alone. His wife told him to go first so that he could apply for the whole family to join him. When the transfer order came they knew their days were numbered. He had completely lost his will power; he just let the two women struggle for him, ready to accept the arrangements of Fate. It looked as if his wife was going to win, but she speeded up her attack, meeting him almost daily. They met far away from the city, on the other side of the railway. She begged him: "Don't go, please don't go!"

He only held her and cried.

Her husband decided to act. That night he brought a dozen men with him, all on their bikes, and they followed them to their meeting place. They surrounded them and caught them. They beat him and held her to make her look. At first she would not look, and then she looked straight at them beating him and wailed. Her husband was crying in his heart too, crying because she was crying, and crying because he had to punish her like this. By punishing her he was admitting the fact that she was unfaithful to him! He remained silent while they beat him; he had lost consciousness. The sound of her crying seemed to come from a long way off; it was unreal. She wailed bitterly, and then her tears ran dry and she stared with dry, wide-open eyes. There was a look of excitement and desperation in her eyes which frightened even her husband. A train thundered by. They finally stopped the beating and let him go.

He stumbled along the railway until he reached a barrier gate where he realized that he was heading in the wrong direction and turned back again. He did not get home until one in the morning. From his depressed and desperate look his wife saw everything. She did not question him, just helped him onto the bed. His cold body began to shiver, as if he had malaria, and the whole bed shook. She suppressed the bitterness in her heart and took him into her arms, calling silently for him to show some sign of life, trying hopelessly to revive him with the warmth of her body. Lying in her warm embrace, his cold body shivered even more violently, and instead of keeping him warm, she too turned cold. They lay there in the coldness for the whole night; he was dead to the world but she did not even close her eyes.

The sky was blue, with not even a trace of a cloud. The sun was shining brightly. It was another Sunday. She thought shakily: It's a good omen.

He had also woken up, and was sitting dully in bed. After a while he got up, folded the quilt and made the bed. At breakfast she asked him tentatively,

"Going out today?"

He shook his head and then said, "I'll wash the floor."

She left him alone while he brought a pail of water and a mop to wash the rough concrete floor. When he had finished he leaned on the bed and read. The sun was shining in warmly through the window, straight onto his face, but he did not notice. She went over and lowered the bamboo blind, feeling gradually more at ease and went to do the laundry. Then it occurred to her that they had not been to the market yet and asked him to go. He answered her call at once, went out obediently with some money and the shopping basket. She told him to put on a shirt but he said it was just a short distance and it was warm, so he went out wearing a pair of trousers, a vest, and his sandals.

He walked under the sun. What happened the night before was like a dream, or something from another life. He had lost all sensation and all feeling; he walked on numbly, like the living dead. He felt extremely insignificant; the crowd pushed at him and he was helpless. He walked from one end of the market to the other, not buying much. At this time she was looking all over town for him.

She was looking for him and she had to find him. She had come out early in the morning wearing a white seersucker dress. She had cut up all her other clothes; she had spent the whole night cutting them to pieces. Her husband did not go home with her. He was dragged off by his friends who were afraid that he might kill her. She was left alone.

At last she saw him at the crossroads near the market. He was walking leisurely carrying a shopping basket. She stopped him. He stood still, looking at her in a daze.

"Come with me," she said.

And he followed her, still carrying his shopping basket.

"Come quickly," she turned back and called for him tearfully.

He stepped up his pace, still carrying his shopping basket.

They were not afraid of being seen anymore; they did not avoid anyone. And strangely people did not seem to recognize them; no one was watching them. People were bustling, enjoying a happy Sunday. They walked on unhindered towards the north.

She was walking faster and faster.

Gradually he found it hard to catch up with her and he dropped his basket without realizing it. The things he had bought were scattered all over the ground, but no one noticed.

They had left the crowds far behind and had reached the countryside. Slowly they drew close and were walking together.

"You don't regret coming with me, do you?" She asked him, trying to hold back her tears. A teardrop hung on her eye lashes, like a pearl.

He smiled and shook his head. Now he was just like a blade of withered grass, drifting rootlessly in the wind, with no will of its own.

"If we can't live together we will die together," she said firmly. The teardrop was glittering. She had grown thin and was not full-fleshed anymore. Her bones showed now, but this gave her an ethereal beauty.

They came to the foot of the barren mountain and began to climb. She was wearing a pair of white high-heeled shoes which made the upward climb easy, and gradually he fell behind. She turned back and gave him her hand, saying tenderly, "Come." At her tender summons his soul flew out to her.

They came to the stretch of grassland where they had been before. The grass was still yellow and the sun had not reached there. She helped him sit down and held him like a baby, rubbing her cheeks against his. After they had caressed for a while she took a small bottle from her white handbag, broke the seal and fed him the contents. He drank obediently, without asking what it was. She threw away the empty bottle, petted his face encouragingly, took out another bottle and fed it to him. She gave him seven bottles, and then she started taking them herself. She seemed to be impatient and broke the seals with her teeth, swallowing the liquid together with the broken glass. She too took seven bottles. And then she took out a ball of wool made of colourful lengths twined together.

"Hold me by the neck," she whispered tenderly.

He held her by the neck, his soft arms wrapping around it. He felt it was like holding onto his mother's neck when he was very, very young.

She tied their bodies together. She wound the wool round and round, and asked him gently, "Does it hurt?"

He shook his head limply. She kissed him.

She had come to the end of the string. She tied a fast knot using her mouth and hand, and then she said softly, "Now, lie down."

They fell together onto the cool, soft grass.

His mind began to wander. He saw his grandfather's aquiline nose and shiny eyes which blinked at him triumphantly, and then it was replaced by a gentle look which seemed to beckon him, and so he went. But he also felt that he was walking behind his brother on the busy Huaihai Road in Shanghai; the fragrance of cream cakes came to his nostrils. The siren sounded at the pier, so loudly that it shook the sky. It was mingled with the exercise tune for the cello, the one that went two steps forward and one step back, climbing up and down the scale. Rays of sunlight shone into the little wood and turned into moonlight which gently caressed him — it was his daughter's hand. And then the flames flooded everything, flames that were growing fiercer and fiercer, and the colour became darker and darker until it was total blackness. When life began in a mother's womb it must have been as black as this. He felt protected and secure now, and he smiled.

Her mind was also wandering, but she saw only clothes. Red, orange, yellow, blue, purple, dark and pale green. A quilted floral coat with pretty piping, little shoes embroidered with mandarin ducks, bell-bottomed trousers, pink elasticated stockings, a silvery white western suit that fitted tightly around the waist, long flowing gowns, so colourful and so rich.... Her tears fell; they rolled over the mole by her ear and fell to the ground, like pearls.

CHAPTER FOUR

XXXVII

After seven days and seven nights a group of students came to the city on holiday and went to see the mountain.

Their clamour frightened all the birds away.

They combed the barren mountain trying without success to find somewhere interesting. But on a piece of flat land on the western side they found a number of shiny little bottles, and then they saw in the grass four entangled legs and like the frightened birds they rushed downhill screaming and shouting.

XXXVIII

His brother came all the way from Shanghai to see to his funeral. He looked at his brother wrapped in a bundle of white cloth and thought: Would it have been better if he had not taken him away to school? It also occurred to him that the two brothers he took with him both died young. One of them died of an illness, it was his fate and it could not have been prevented, but the other one, could that also be fate? He did not know, nevertheless he felt guilty.

XXXIX

His wife could not even cry. She was filled with hate and bitterness and regret. If they had not come here none of this would have happened. But they did come, and that was that.

Strangely his wife did not really hate her now, though she knew he could not have hardened himself to do this had it not been for her. She also knew that there was nothing in this world that held him back from doing it but his cowardice. She knew this man too well. She did not hate him either. These few years, these few decades had been too hard on him. She could not love him enough.

XL

His mother had grown so deaf that for a long time she could not hear the sirens. And then one day the sound of the sirens blasted continuously in her ears, so loudly that it tore her heart.

She seemed to have been given a clue. From then on she never mentioned his name and never asked any questions. No one needed to take care of her.

XLI

The girl's mother did not cry. She thought: Her daughter had found her one and only man; not only did they meet but they talked, they understood each other and they went together. Who knows, perhaps that was a blessing.

XLII

The next year the grass on the western side of the mountain was lush green.

XLIII

....

RENDITIONS PAPERBACKS

Xi Xi: *A Girl Like Me & Other Stories*
ISBN 962-201-382-1   US$6.95   £3.95

Yu Luojin: *A Chinese Winter's Tale*
ISBN 962-201-383-X   US$9.50   £5.95

Tao Yang: *Borrowed Tongue*
ISBN 962-201-381-3   US$9.50   £5.95

David Hawkes: *A Little Primer of Tu Fu*
ISBN 962-7255-02-5   US$9.50   £5.95

Wang Anyi: *Love in a Small Town*
ISBN 962-7255-03-3   US$8.50   £4.95

A Golden Treasury of Chinese Poetry
ISBN 962-7255-04-1   US$10.50   £6.95

Gu Cheng: *Selected Poems*
ISBN 962-7255-05-X   US$9.50   £5.95

Liu Xinwu: *Black Walls & Other Stories*
ISBN 962-7255-06-8   US$9.50   £5.95

Li Yu: *Silent Operas*
ISBN 962-7255-07-6   US$10.95   £6.95

Contemporary Women Writers: Hong Kong & Taiwan
ISBN 962-7255-08-4   US$10.50   £5.95

Mo Yan: *Explosions & Other Stories*
ISBN 962-7255-10-5   US$10.50   £6.95

Han Shaogong: *Homecoming? & Other Stories*
ISBN 962-7255-13-0   US$10.95   £6.95

Orders and enquiries to:
Renditions, Chinese University of Hong Kong, Shatin, NT., Hong Kong
Tel: (852) 609-7407   Fax: (852) 603-5149

RENDITIONS PAPERBACKS

Contemporary Women Writers: Hong Kong and Taiwan
ISBN 962-7255-08-4   US$10.50   £5.95

Seven stories by prominent authors explore changing attitudes and issues facing modern women from two Chinese experiences.

Xi Xi: *A Girl Like Me & Other Stories*
ISBN 962-201-382-1   US$6.95   £3.95

Haunting and lyrical stories by Hong Kong's most accomplished woman writer, whose style reflects Hong Kong's unique fusion of East and West, tradition and modernity.

Yu Luojin: *A Chinese Winter's Tale*
ISBN 962-201-383-X   US$9.50   £5.95

Widely read and highly controversial in the author's homeland, this is an intensely personal account of a young woman's experiences in the Cultural Revolution, as well as a compelling social document.

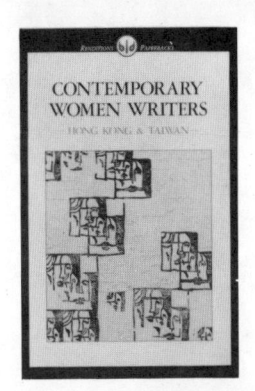

Renditions, Chinese University of Hong Kong, Shatin, NT., Hong Kong
Tel (852) 609-7407   Fax (852) 603-5149